An Augathella Surprise

ANNIE SEATON

Augathella Short and Sweets: 1

ISBN 978-1-923048-10-2

Dedication

This book is dedicated to my dear readers.

You wanted more of the 'girls'.

Here is a new series!

AUGATHELLA SHORT AND SWEETS

An Augathella Surprise

An Augathella Baby

An Augathella Wedding

An Augathella Winter

An Augathella Ball

An Augathella Spring

An Augathella Christmas

Following on from:

THE AUGATHELLA GIRLS

Book 1: Outback Roads –The Nanny
Book 2: Outback Sky – The Pilot
Book 3: Outback Escape – The Sister
Book 4: Outback Winds – The Jillaroo
Book 5: Outback Dawn – The Visitor
Book 6: Outback Moonlight – The Rogue
Book 7: Outback Dust – The Drifter
Book 8: Outback Hope – The Farmer

Chapter 1

Gold Coast Weddings -Chapel of Love

'Move away. Give her some space.' Jenna Wilson stepped forward as the bride dissolved into a fresh round of gasping sobs. 'Listen up everyone, how about we all step out for a minute and let Rina compose herself?'

'Don't you friggin' tell me what to do. She's *my* friend and my sister-in-law-to-be.' A tall woman with dark hair shoved Jenna, and she had to grab for the counter of the vanity as she tottered on her high heels. It didn't help that the floor was wet and slippery from a leaking tap at the end of the row of basins. This wedding venue was nowhere near as upmarket as Jenna had expected when she'd been invited to her boss's wedding.

'Excuse me!' Jenna's best friend, Alana Rickman, pushed through the melee of women filling the small restroom. 'You almost knocked my friend over.'

'I don't give a flying fig what I did. She doesn't tell us what to do. Rina, sweetie, come here.' The dark-haired woman tried to put her arms around the sobbing bride. 'Jock'll be okay in a minute. They're pouring coffee into him now.'

'Leave me alone, Diane.' The bride stepped away from the bossy woman. 'I'm not marrying your brother. Not today, not *ever*.'

'Come on, sweetie. He's only had a couple

of beers.'

From what Jenna had seen as the groom lurched out of the gents' restroom in the foyer of the wedding venue, he had a lot more than two beers under his belt.

Alana, who'd agreed to come to the wedding with her, had nudged Jenna as they crossed the foyer towards the chapel. 'Get a load of that,' she'd whispered.

Jenna's eyes widened as she turned.

A man with a bare chest, his pants around his knees, seemed unaware that a trail of toilet paper hung from the back of his Calvin Kleins as he lurched towards the chapel. He was muttering but his words were slurred and impossible to understand. Two guys in suits hurried after him.

'Jocko, stop!' A burly guy with tattoos circling his neck and on the back of his shaved head grabbed for the man.

A couple of the female guests tried to distract the bride when she'd come through the main door with her two bridesmaids. Jenna's mouth fell open in shock as her elegant boss spotted him before he fell to the floor, a happy grin gracing his face.

It hadn't been until Rina screamed and ran for the ladies' room, followed by most of the women who were in the foyer, that Jenna had realised the comatose guy on the floor was the groom.

She couldn't believe her eyes. Rina, the bride and her work supervisor at the premier real estate agency at Surfers Paradise was always stylish and cultured. Word was she'd moved to the Gold Coast from Double Bay in Sydney and had been part of the social set in the city.

Jenna had expected Sydney socialites at the wedding, but the group of wedding guests—to put it politely—were a tad rough around the edges. The venue had surprised her too; it was tired and tatty, and she'd noticed a mouldy smell in the foyer as she and Alana waited to go into the chapel before the ruckus started.

'Next time you ask me to come and keep you company at a wedding, I'll think twice,' Alana said, shaking her head as the tattooed man crouched over the groom.

'I don't believe you,' Jenna said. 'You're a serial wedding guest. Nothing keeps you away from weddings. You love them. That's why when it said "plus guest" on my invite, I thought of you straight away.'

'You need to find yourself a man. I keep telling you that.' Jenna nudged her with a grin.

The two girls had been friends since the first year of high school, and now they caught up at least once a week since Alana had moved to Burleigh Heads. They were polar opposites;

Jenna was career-oriented, and Alana flitted from one job to another on her perpetual search for Mr Right, but Alana had been good for Jenna. She'd taught Jenna to chill and not focus so much on trying to climb the career ladder. If Jenna was honest, she hadn't been getting as much satisfaction out of her job lately.

'Although this is almost enough to turn a girl off getting married.' Alana's grin was cheeky. 'But you know me, Jen, I'm always on the hunt for my perfect groom.'

'I do know you.' Jenna had tried not to chuckle. 'I'd say the guy on the floor is far from perfect. Come on, I'll go and check that Rina's okay, and then we might head to the pub. What do you think?'

'We're too dressed up for the pub. How about we go to the Sheraton? My shout.'

'Sounds like a plan.' Alana followed her across to the ladies' room. 'By the look of the groom, I don't think there's going to be a wedding this afternoon.'

When they entered the ladies' restroom, Jenna couldn't believe the scene that greeted them. Rina was hanging onto the side of the vanity, her head over the basin. Another friend had come in with two glasses of champagne and was trying to push one into the bride's face.

'No,' Rina yelled. 'I don't want it. Just everybody get out of here. Let me catch my breath, and then I'm going home.'

'You can't go home, sweetie. You're getting married,' one of the fuchsia-pink-clad bridesmaids piped up.

Rina straightened, her eyes widening. 'You're right, I can't. I'm not going home because I'm never going to go back to his apartment again.'

'Aw, come on, sweetie. You've got to get married. Jock is waiting for you.'

'Waiting for me? Prostrate drunk with no pants on, out in the foyer? You must be joking,' Rina said. The culture had come back into her voice a little bit as the immediate shock wore off. 'I'm a laughing stock already.'

Jenna stepped forward. 'If you're serious, Rina, I can give you a lift back to wherever you want to go,' she said quietly.

The pushy woman stepped in front of Jenna. 'No, you piss off, bitch. Rina is marrying my brother. He'll get himself together in a minute. Rina honey, scull your champers. Come on, pull yourself together, and wash your face.' She waved a huge hairbrush in front of the bride's face. 'I'll help you get your hair tidy again.'

'Diane, I am not marrying your brother. In fact, if that's what the thought of getting married can do to someone they're supposed to love, I'm not ever marrying anyone. He needed a skinful of grog to go through with the wedding. So just get out of my way. I'm leaving. Now.'

Jenna didn't see the punch coming as she stepped closer to Rina. The next thing she knew, her face was aching against the cold tiles of the restroom floor. Her ears were ringing, and Rina was screaming, 'Diane, you're as bad as your stupid brother! Just look at what you've done to poor Jenna!'

Alana crouched next to her. 'Oh my God, Jen, are you okay? Do I need to call an ambulance? Did you hit your head?'

Jenna's face was aching and her right wrist was throbbing. She'd managed to break her fall with her right arm, and for a moment, she thought she'd broken it. She flexed her wrist gingerly. 'No, I'm fine. Let's just get the hell out of here.'

As Alana helped her to her feet, Jenna leaned against the wall. Her head was spinning, and she put one hand on her cheek. 'I'm not bleeding, am I? I hope I don't have any broken teeth.'

Voices were rising, and there was a lot of pushing and shoving going on as the groom's family tried to persuade Rina to stay, and her friends tried to get her to leave.

'No, there's just a red mark there. Come on, let's get out of here before this turns into a brawl.'

Rina screamed from behind, 'Jen, wait! I'm so sorry! Don't go.'

'It's okay, Rina. It wasn't you.' Jenna glared at the woman who apparently was going to be the sister-in-law-no-more. She shook her head. 'I might even go to the police station and press charges,' she said as the woman made a rude gesture.

Alana held her arm as they walked across the car park. 'Well, that was fun. Do you want to go to the pub or home?'

'Do I look okay? I'd love a drink.'

'You look fine. As long as you feel okay.'

'Good. Let's go.' Alana's eyebrows rose in question. 'The police station first?'

'No, I was just trying to wind her up. Besides poor Rina was wound up enough without the police arriving. Let's get out of this place.'

Chapter 2

Callie Cartwright leaned back on the soft cushions of the new sofa she and Braden had bought in Charleville a couple of weeks ago. She sighed with pleasure as her husband's strong fingers massaged her bare feet. The room was warm from the crackling fire in the slow-combustion stove, and she closed her eyes and murmured, 'I didn't think those three boys were ever going to go to sleep tonight.'

'It's all your fault,' Braden said, grinning at her. 'You brought up the choice of the baby's name over dinner.'

'It did lead to a bit of a discussion,' she said with a grin.

'It sure did. I quite like "Muesli".' Braden chuckled.

'Our child is *not* going to be called "Muesli", no matter how much Petie wants it.' Callie sat up straight but she couldn't help giggling. 'Although he was really cross when we said no. First time I've ever seen him storm off to his room.'

'It was more like a Nigel tantrum than Petie's usual behaviour, but he did come back when the ice cream came out,' Braden replied. 'I think he's been a bit spoiled and we've let him have his own way too much since he came home from hospital.'

'Maybe. But oh, sweetheart, how wonderful is it to see him running around with the other pair as though he never had that awful accident.'

'It is, despite all the new grey hairs I gained in those weeks.' Braden moved up the sofa next to Callie and rested his chin on top of her head. 'But there's no way he's getting his way this time. "Muesli" Cartwright? Not a chance.' His chest rumbled against her as he laughed.

'Nigel was closer to the mark with Malachi. What is it with all the M words anyway? Rory wanted Michael.'

'I could live with Michael,' Braden said.

'Fifty-fifty chance it's a girl. How about Megan? I quite like that.'

'How about Melody?' Braden asked.

'No, not a fan.'

'Anyway, I'm sure there's a big boy growing in there.' Braden put his hand on Callie's huge stomach and shook his head. 'If it's a girl she'll be playing for the Augathella Meat Ants, my sweet.'

Callie shook her head. 'It's a girl, and I don't know about her playing football.'

'Will we have a bet?' Braden's grin was

wide and Callie snuggled closer—as best as she could—and her heart filled with love for this strong, wonderful man.

If anyone had told her eighteen months ago where she would be now, and how happy she would be, she would never have believed them. Living on a cattle station in the western outback, far away from all that was familiar to her, with a gorgeous husband and three adorable stepsons, and back in the classroom part-time, she would have laughed. Even going worldwide on TikTok with that embarrassing incident on the weather network had been worth it, because it had sent her fleeing to the outback and she had been rescued by Braden.

'Your appointment in Charleville is next week, isn't it?' he said, interrupting her musing. 'Tell me again what the obstetrician said when you went down to see him last month.'

Callie opened her eyes and lifted her head.

Braden was looking at her with a concerned look on his face.

'Stop worrying. He told me everything is fine. All those minor issues that I've had have all sorted themselves out. My blood pressure is perfect. The baby is the right size, and the heartbeat is nice and strong.'

'It's a bugger that we're mustering next week. Do you really think you should be driving?' Braden asked.

'Of course I can drive,' Callie reassured him, reaching out and pushing a loose strand of hair back from his forehead. 'You need a haircut.'

'I know I do, but we've just been so busy with the mustering, there's been little time for anything. It's nice to be home with you tonight. I'm just glad Jon's here to help us this month. Once he takes over his own property after the sale goes through, he's going to be pretty busy down there. And Fallon's busy with little Ryan, so she won't be flying helicopters for a while. I know Kent's got onto a new helicopter pilot from down in the Channel Country, and he's coming up to see us next week, but we're on horseback and our bikes until we see if he can help out. It's been such a great season. I still can't believe how healthy the cattle are,' Braden said.

'That's good. Healthy cattle, better prices?'

'You're turning into a station wife, Cal. And yes, it's going to be a good year financially.'

'That's good to hear. Did I tell you I looked at prams when I was down in Charleville last month?' she asked.

'No, you didn't. Did you order one?'

'No, I didn't. They were too expensive.' Callie shook her head. 'I was going to look online.'

'So, what are you going to do? Carry the

new bub around all the time and not have a pram? Don't be silly,' Braden said.

'Yeah, but the one I liked was over a thousand dollars!'

'Less than the price of a beast,' Braden stated matter-of-factly. 'Order it.'

'Are you sure?'

'Of course I'm sure. If you order it tomorrow, you can pick it up when you go down next week. How often do you have to go down after the next visit?'

'I'm on weekly visits after that, so five weeks to go. Five weeks and our baby will be here,' Callie calculated.

Braden chuckled. 'You know what I'm thinking?'

'What?' she asked with a frown.

'Muesli Sylvia Cartwright does have a nice ring to it, don't you think?'

'If you want "Muesli" I'll buy the two-thousand-dollar pram!' Callie reached across and tickled him.

'Okay, time we went to bed, Mrs Cartwright. I've got an early start tomorrow,' Braden said, standing up and holding out his hand to help her to her feet. 'I haven't told you today how much I love you, have I, Callie Cartwright?'

'No, you haven't, Braden, but I'm happy for you to tell me again,' Callie said with a smile.

Chapter 3

Jenna came out of the ladies' powder room of the Sheraton restroom feeling a lot better. She'd washed her face, examined the red mark on her cheek and camouflaged it with more makeup, fluffed her hair up, and if you hadn't known she'd just face-planted onto the tiles at the wedding centre, you'd never have guessed it had happened.

Alana passed her a glass of bubbles when she climbed onto the barstool beside her. 'Cheers, girlfriend! That was the shortest wedding I've ever been to.'

Jenna shook her head. 'I still can't believe

what happened.'

'I thought you said your boss was elegant.'

'Well, she's always very well-spoken and often speaks about her time in Sydney when we have morning tea in the office. She was so different today.'

'I'm sure I've seen some of those guys before. The ones who were hovering outside when we came out. Those guys belong to a motorcycle club,' Alana said. 'They used to come to the Burleigh pub where I worked.'

'Oh well, it was nothing like I imagined, but what an experience.' Jenna sighed. 'It'll be interesting to see what happens in a couple of weeks when Rina comes back from her two weeks off. They were supposed to be going to the Cook Islands for the honeymoon. I wonder if she'll change her mind and marry him.'

'You know, once he sobers up, they'll probably make up, run away somewhere and get married, and then have the honeymoon. Love's a strange thing.' Alana rolled her eyes. 'Not that I know.'

Jenna sipped from her glass and the bubbles tickled her nose. 'You try too hard, Alana. You're happy in your new job, aren't you?'

Alana pulled a face. 'Not really. I've got a bit bored down here on the Gold Coast. I'm thinking about moving west.'

'Moving west? Why would you do that?'

Alana grinned. 'I thought I could set my sights on some rich cow cocky.'

Jenna widened her eyes, and she couldn't help the laughter spilling from her lips. 'You marry a cow cocky? Have you ever even been to the country, girl?'

'I went there once when I was a kid. Mum and Dad took me out to Toowoomba.'

Jenna shook her head. 'Alana, that's not the country. Toowoomba is a city.'

'Well, I'm thinking about looking for a job out that way. Anyway, I'll get to one of those B and S balls. They seem to have lots of single blokes there.'

'You try too hard, Alana. Marriage isn't the be-all and end-all. We've got a life to live before all that happens. Go overseas, have great holidays, and have no responsibility.'

'It's all right for you with your swanky real estate office job and your degree behind you. Being a waitress doesn't pay that much. I'm hardly saving, and I don't like the new job much.'

Jenna looked at her friend over the rim of her glass. She knew that Alana was speaking from her heart. She might change jobs and find another one on the coast and she'd be happy again for a few weeks. It was sad that she felt as though she needed to have an engagement ring on her finger.

'Don't get offended, but I think you come on a bit heavy talking about the future on your first couple of dates.'

'I know, but I want to make it clear that's what I'm after.'

'And they run a mile?'

Alana nodded sadly. 'They do.'

'I rest my case. Have you been back on that dating app lately?' Jenna asked.

'Don't talk about it. Let's have another drink.'

Chapter 4

The two weeks that Rina had been away from work had increased Jenna's workload considerably. The day Rina was due back, Jenna arrived in the office early so that she could get everything up to date and have the new files moved across to the shared folder that Rina would access. Three contracts needed to be finalised today, and Jenna made sure that they were printed out, slipped into plastic sleeves labelled with the clients' names and placed on Rina's desk.

Jenna had closed on a particularly good sale,

one of the units at the new complex on the Isle of Capri. They were so hard to come by, and when she had been the agent who had finalised the sale, she knew that the commission would go towards the holiday she'd been talking to Alana about last weekend.

Alana had left her job as Jenna had known she would, and now she was working in a small fish and chip shop at Broadbeach and was already saying how much she hated it.

Jenna understood Alana had a tremendous work ethic and was really smart, but she didn't seem to have the confidence to go for the bigger jobs.

Jenna focused on her work as she heard a lift ding outside her office. Rina pushed the door open; she was dressed immaculately in a red silk suit with her signature Jimmy Choos making her about ten centimetres taller.

Alana stood to greet her, and Rina glanced

across at her with a brittle smile. 'I'd like to meet with you in my office at nine o'clock, please, Miss Wilson.'

That was a bit strange. Jenna pulled a face and glanced at her watch; it was fifteen minutes away.

She'd just have time to make a quick cup of coffee, touch up her lipstick, and be on time for the appointment. She felt unsettled; the woman who had just walked into the office was very different from the devastated bride she had left at the wedding centre two weeks ago.

There had been no news in the office as to what had happened, and Jenna had been the only one from the real estate agency invited to the wedding. She'd been surprised when she received the invitation but had been keen to go along. However, it had been such a fiasco, she pushed it out of her mind. Alana hadn't mentioned it again either. She'd been too caught up in her own woes.

Right on the dot of nine o'clock, Jenna stood. She walked across to the other side of the office. Rina's receptionist, Cathy, gave her a cool glance. 'Miss Wilson, please take a seat.'

Jenna went to say something; she knew Cathy quite well, but when Cathy turned back to her computer she shrugged and sat down.

A moment later, the phone on Cathy's desk buzzed. 'Rina is ready now, go in, please.'

Jenna walked into Rina's office and waited to be asked to sit down. This was obviously a formal meeting, so she treated it as such.

Rina walked around the side of her desk, the glass wall behind her providing a panoramic vista of the beach at Surfers Paradise. 'Jenna,' she said.

For a moment, Jenna wondered if she should ask how she was, but no, Rina wasn't very receptive this morning. As she stood there waiting to be invited to sit down, her boss reached over for an envelope and passed it across to her as she stood there. 'This is a statement of employment for any future employer, Jenna. Unfortunately, we have to terminate your services.'

Jenna's stomach sank like a lead balloon, and she stood there in disbelief looking at Rina.

'Your performance hasn't been up to what we wanted at this agency, Jenna.'

'But my figures have—'

'Please don't interrupt me. You haven't reached your marketing target for the year.'

'We're only three months into the financial year,' Jenna protested. 'And I—' The unfairness of what Rina was saying burned in Jenna's chest.

Rina waved a dismissive hand. 'Please don't argue. I've discussed this with Bob, and we've decided to let you go. Your final payment, your severance payment, has already been paid into your account. An email of how it's been worked out has been sent to your personal account. Your business email account has been terminated. If you have any problems, you know the accountant's number. Please call our accountant, and he'll talk you through it. I'll also remind you that you signed an agreement not to contact any of your former clients should you leave the agency.'

'You can't do that,' Jenna said. 'I *have* met my marketing targets.'

Suddenly the penny dropped. 'This is because I saw what happened at your wedding!'

'We won't go there, Jenna, and I'd appreciate it if you don't share what occurred on that afternoon. I've moved on now, and I'm sorry, but as I said, your marketing achievements are not up to what we want.'

Anger bubbled in Jenna's stomach, and she

stepped forward, gripping the chair in front of her so tightly it moved forward and scraped on the white tiles. 'So that's it?' she ground out.

Rina's eyebrows raised, and her stare was glacial. 'Yes, that's it. Welcome to the world of big business, Jenna.'

'No, I won't accept this. I have worked my butt off for this agency for the last three years. In the last two weeks while you were away, I—'

Rina had the upper hand. 'I've seen what you've done in the last two weeks, and that was a little bit better. Well done. I ensured that the commission has been added to your payout, as you'll see when you check your email. Your personal email. Please clear out your desk and leave immediately.'

Chapter 5

Three weeks later, after Jenna had given a lot of thought to what had happened at the wedding that never was, and the subsequent meeting with Rina, she walked out of her solicitor's office.

The new paralegal at her regular solicitors had been a cute guy, and he'd asked her for a date on the way out from her appointment. She shook her head. 'No, thank you. I'm moving away.'

He shrugged. 'Fair enough.'

She did feel bad about being a bit too dismissive. Alana was the one with the burning desire to partner up and get married. Jenna had visions of living in her new home, and having a happy life by herself.

It wasn't just the wedding and being laid off that had woken her up to where she really wanted to be. It was the whole city thing on the Gold Coast. The crowds, the crime, the tourists and the false glitziness of the social scene. Not to mention the business environment that had let her down.

She and Alana had caught up for coffee a week after the wedding when Jenna's black eye had faded, and she felt like she could go out in public again. She had taken a couple of sick leave days and it had given her a lot of time to think about her future. Maybe she'd look for something else, the cutthroat workplace environment in the world of real estate was wearing thin. She had Granny's inheritance carefully invested, and as she'd walked out of

Rina's office an idea began to form.

A total change of scene and she could start the business she'd always dreamed of.

Definitely not on the Gold Coast. Maybe she could start her vintage tea room in the hinterland of the Sunshine Coast?

Jenna spent the first week of being unemployed looking for cottages on land in the country. After seeing the price of real estate on the coast, her search took her further west. She could imagine a cute little country cottage on an acre of gardens, and maybe if she went further west, she could afford what she was looking for. By the end of the second week of searching her search had taken her way out west. Seven hundred kilometres to be exact.

She hadn't mentioned it to Alana when they'd caught up for coffee the other day, but they were meeting for a drink tonight, and she was going to break the news that she'd been sacked—because that was the only word for the way she'd been treated—and that she'd found the perfect location for her new venture.

Excitement trickled through her. Maybe Alana would come with her; it would be great if she had company to start up her business, but if not, she would make the most of it. She was sure there were people out there who were looking for a job.

'Hey Jen, how's it going?' Alana stood as Jenna walked across the bar. She ignored the few interested looks thrown her way.

'I'm good. How are you?' Jen greeted her friend.

'The usual.' Alana pulled a face. 'Not good.'

Jenna raised her eyebrows. 'How come? Not enough business at the fish and chip shop?'

'No, I left there last week and started a new job. Didn't I tell you? A swanky restaurant.'

'And you don't like it?'

'I *loved* it! But I got the sack.'

'They sacked you? Why?'

'Yep. The excuse was that they had enough staff already, but I overheard a conversation on my second night. The boss said I wasn't elegant enough and that hurt. I took the next day off sick but I decided to stick it out and then he told me he was overstaffed.'

'Have you been sick?'

'No, I just didn't want to work there after what I heard, but then I changed my mind. I'm totally over the Gold Coast. I'm thinking about going back to Gympie.'

'Do you really want to go home?' Jenna stared at Alana, hope flaring. 'I've got some news. I'm moving too,' she said.

'You sold your apartment?'

'No, I was only renting.'

'Oh, I thought it was yours,' Alana said.

'You're moving to a new one?'

'No. Not only did I get the sack too, I've bought a house, and I'm going to start the business I've always wanted.'

'Hang on, let's rewind here. You got the sack too?'

'Yes, apparently Rina didn't like me witnessing her wedding fiasco.'

'So, she sacked you?' Alana's voice was full of indignation. 'What a bitch. She can't do that.'

'Probably not, but I'm really pleased. It's forced me to do what I've always wanted to. Buy a cottage and start a vintage tea room.'

'My God, Jenna! Did you win the lottery?'

'No, I got a good payout from the company and I added it to some money I inherited from my gran, and I've found the place I want to buy. I've been to see the solicitor today and I signed the contract.'

'Lucky you. I'd like to move too, but if I go back to Gympie, which I probably will, I'll have to stay at Mum and Dad's.'

'Why do you want to go back there?'

'I'm over the busyness of this place,' Alana said. 'I'm over working for dickheads, and I'd like to go back to where I grew up. Life is slower there, less hectic, and you don't have to try to measure up all the time. It's just that I don't suit this place, and I know I've been slack taking sickies, but this last time did me a favour. It made me decide.'

'So, you've given up your apartment too?'

Alana nodded. 'I have. I'll be going home in a couple of weeks. I'll miss you, Jen. Can you take me and show me your new house after we have a coffee?'

Jenna chuckled. 'Not really. It's a little way away.'

'How far?'

'Well, about two and a half days' drive west.'

'What? Where the heck are you going?' Alana said.

'I'm starting my own business. I bought a cottage on an acre on the highway at Augathella, and I'm going to start a vintage tea shop.'

'Get out of it! Are you for real?'

'I am.' Jenna looked at her best friend, who had supported her for three years on the coast. 'I'll be looking for staff, and it would help to have someone to help me fix up the place. What do you reckon?'

'It's in the country?'

'It's in the country, that's for sure,' Jenna said.

'And you want staff, and you want someone to help you fix up the place.'

'I do.'

'Where would I live?'

'It's quite a big cottage. The tearoom will go into the current living room and dining room, and there's still room to live at the back. It does need some work before I can open the business. I'll definitely have to add a small powder room for the customers but from the pictures...'

Alana interrupted. 'What do you mean, from the pictures? You haven't seen it? You haven't been out there?'

'No, I bought it on spec,' she said. 'I looked at the pictures and the surrounding area. It's on the highway. It's going to have a captive audience of grey nomads as they go past. I've looked at the tourism figures, and I've done a feasibility study and a business plan, and I reckon I can build a really successful business in a cute little town. I need a hand, though. What do you reckon?'

'When do we move? Alana's features spread

into a wide grin.

'Two weeks.'

'Count me in, girlfriend.' She high-fived Jenna. 'Hang on, where are we moving to?'

'Augathella,' Jenna said with a big smile.

Chapter 6

Reg closed the door of his house and sat down on the rickety chair on the veranda before setting off on his morning walk to the pub. Like he had every morning since he'd come home from his job out in the bush a few years back. He'd moved back into the house that had been in his family for almost a hundred years. Reg looked down at the floor. It needed a bit of work these days. The chair leg of the other chair had gone through the timber at the end of the veranda last week, and he stayed away from that end. The last thing he wanted to do was fall over and break something looking like an old codger.

He couldn't believe it when someone from Charleville Real Estate called and said they had an offer on his house. Who the heck would want to come and buy this old place? It was falling down around him. He thought someone would buy it and bulldoze it to run cattle. He always hoped that Polly Jones who owned the land next door would take the hint and buy the extra bit of land, but no matter how much he hinted, she'd never been interested.

Some woman had bought it, and he had to go down and sign the papers at the real estate agent tomorrow. When Callie Cartwright heard he was looking for a lift down and back, she'd offered to drive him to Charleville because she had a doctor's appointment there. She and Braden and the three little boys had been there for dinner last night, and she always talked to him. When he told her he had to find a way to Charleville tomorrow, she'd offered straight away.

He looked at her and his forehead wrinkled in a frown. 'You won't pop that baby out on the way, will you?'

'No, Reg. I still have four weeks to go.'

'Should you be driving that great big Land Cruiser of yours?'

Callie laughed, and he thought again what a lovely smile she had. It reminded him of Margie's smile. He had a soft spot for Callie since she moved to town a couple of years back, for that very reason.

'I will give you one thing. It's getting a bit hard to climb up into. I've got to pull myself up like an old lady,' she said. 'But don't worry, there is an alternative.'

'Well, love, if you're offering to take me down, I wouldn't mind a bit of company on the way. That would be really good.'

'Where do you have to go to?' she asked.

'I have to go to the lawyer's office, and I have to do a bit of shopping.' He didn't tell her what for, but if he was going to the aged care place, he'd have to get some pyjamas.

Callie looked at him curiously but didn't ask, and he appreciated that. He was a private bloke, and he didn't want everyone to know his business. He'd been into what he'd once called "the old people's home" when the lawyer fellow sent him a letter saying the sale was going through. These days he reckoned "aged care" had a nicer ring to it.

Matron Ramsay, who he'd known since she was a whipper snapper had looked at him with a nod. 'Well, Reg, you must've known something. We've got two places. We've got a room where you can go to the dining room and be totally looked after. Or we've got an independent living unit where you look after yourself.'

'I'll take the room,' he said. 'Who carked it?'

'Carked it?' Matron looked horrified. 'Oh no, Reg. Nobody's passed away. Mr and Mrs Fuller have decided to move to the aged care facility in Charleville to be closer to their children, and Bonnie Dwyer has gone to Newcastle in New South Wales to be closer to her sister. We just happened to have some rooms come available all at once.'

'Where do I sign up?' he said.

'Well, we have to fill out an application form.'

Reg waved a dismissive hand. 'Just do whatever needs to be done. Can you post it down to my solicitor in Charleville? I've got to go down there. He can organise the payment or whatever it is.'

'It's going to be a significant amount, Reg.' The whole town thought he was as poor as a church mouse and that he drank his pension every week.

But they didn't know anything about old Reg MacGilvray.

Chapter 7

'Yes, I let Dad drive my car.' Callie smiled and answered Nigel's question as the three boys sat in the back seat of the Land Cruiser. She soon lost sight of Braden because he was going a lot faster than she was; the red dust billowing out from underneath the wheels of her car were the only sign that he was ahead of them.

When she'd suggested taking her little red sports car down to Charleville this afternoon because it was easier to get into than the Toyota, Braden had readily agreed.

'But you're not driving into town over the corrugated roads. It's too bumpy. At least the

Cruiser's suspension gives you a smooth ride. You can take it in with the boys, while I drive your car in, and then when we get to town, we'll swap over and I'll drop them off at school.'

'And you can help me down out of the car. I can't see Reg doing that.'

'Reg looked like all his Christmases had come at once when he found out you were driving the sports car to Charleville. When you went to round up the boys he said to me, "Not only am I getting a lift to Charleville with the best-looking woman in Augathella, but we're going in her flash red sports car".'

Callie laughed and couldn't wait to see the look on Reg's face when she pulled up at the pub to pick him up.

It was only a short time before Braden turned onto the main highway and headed into Augathella. She followed him to the school at a sedate pace until he pulled up in the back street where there was enough room to park both cars.

'Mum, will you stay parked out here for a while so we can show all our friends your red car?' Rory asked.

'They are going to think it is so way cool.' Nigel grabbed his bag and opened the door of the four-wheel drive. 'Come on, Rory, we'll bring them to the back fence before she can go.'

'Will you wait in it out here for a while so we can get them all to come to the fence and have a look?' Rory begged.

'It's just a car,' Callie replied.

'No, Mum,' said Nigel. 'It's not just a car. Like I said, it's way cool.'

'Can you park it outside kindy too?' Petie asked.

'You stay right there, Peter Cartwright, Braden said through the window. 'I'm dropping you at kindy.'

'I have to leave now to get Reg because we

both have appointments, but when Dad picks you up this afternoon if some of your friends want to see it, we'll wait. But like I said, it's only a car,' Callie said.

Each of the boys leaned forward and kissed her cheek before they climbed out, and a warm glow suffused her.

Braden came to the passenger window after Rory and Nigel had run through the school gate. 'Come on, Callie. I'll help you out.'

Callie picked up her handbag and waited for him to come to the driver's side. She seemed to have doubled in size this week and it was impossible to get in and out of the high car without Braden's help. So, when he'd suggested taking her sports car to Charleville, she jumped at it.

As long as he could put her seat back, she'd be right.

She hoped.

Callie put a hand on her stomach as she waited for Braden. She'd been up all night with heartburn and had thought twice about going down for her obstetrician appointment, but she'd felt better when she woke up. Now her indigestion had come back. She put her hand to her mouth as she let out a small burp.

'Pardon you, Mum,' Petie said from the back seat.

'Yes, pardon me.'

Braden looked at her with concern as he opened the door and held out both hands.

'Are you okay, love?'

'I shouldn't have had that lamb last night,' she said. 'I know exactly what caused it. I don't think your next child likes lamb.'

'That's good. I'm hoping he or she is a beef eater to support the family,' he said with a smile. She swung her legs around to the side and slid down slowly from the driver's seat.

Braden supported her as her feet reached the ground, but her stomach was in the way. He leaned over and kissed her on the neck.

'You drive safely,' he said. 'Don't be tempted to speed.'

'Reg will keep me in line.'

'What's he going to Charleville for?'

Callie shrugged. 'I don't know why, but he has to see his solicitor and do some shopping.'

'He'll be good company for you.'

'It'll be quiet at the pub without him there today,' she said.

'It will, but I'm sure he'll pick up some gossip in Charleville.'

'Bye, Mummy. Drive safe,' Petie parroted his father.

'Bye, sweetie. You be a good boy at kindy.' Callie kissed her fingers and blew the kiss to Petie and he pretended to catch it and throw it back.

'Love you, Mummy.'

'Love you too, Petie.'

Braden waited until Callie put the seat back, and was safely in the sports car before he leaned down and kissed her goodbye. 'You ring me if there are any problems. I'll try to get away from the muster in time to get back here, but if I can't, Jon said Fallon will meet you here at three. Ruth's at their place and can look after Ryan.'

'Bye, sweetheart. You be careful too.' Braden kissed her again and hurried over to the four-wheel drive.

The sports car started with its familiar purr, and Callie smiled as she drove down the street from the school to the pub. She pulled up in the side street and her smile widened as she spotted Reg. Instead of his usual navy-blue King Gee pants and shirt, he was wearing a suit. His white shirt had seen better days, and as he climbed into the front of the car with her, she noticed the yellow, threadbare cuffs and a wave of sympathy ran through her.

Reg was a very private man, and Callie had asked Braden about him, but even though he was a local from way back, no one seemed to know a lot about him.

'I remember first seeing him at the pub when my dad was alive,' Braden said. 'I would've been in primary school, maybe even before then. I remember Mum and Dad talking about him when he first came back to town. Apparently, he was born here, and was a shearer, working around the country, and he was pretty good at it. He won some championships. Anyway, he moved back to town and did some farm stock work out in the bush until he retired.'

'How old is he?' Callie asked.

'I've got no idea, love. I imagine he'd be

heading to eighty if he's not there already. Not a bad innings for someone who sits and drinks beer all day outside the pub.'

'Does he live in town?'

'No, out on the highway. I probably should've pointed his house out to you.'

'On the highway?'

'Yes, just south of town on the way to Charleville.'

'Not that real old place on the western side of the road.'

'That's it.'

'I thought that property was abandoned. Surely, he can't live there?'

Braden nodded. 'He does.'

'But how does he get into town? He hasn't got a car. I mean, he might have a car, but he can't drive into town and drink all day and then drive home.'

'He walks in and out. Gets the occasional

lift, I guess.'

'Really? Oh no, the poor old thing. It must be about five kilometres each way.'

'Probably how he keeps himself fit.'

Callie stared at Reg as he walked across to the car. He was a wiry and fit-looking man for his age.

'Morning, love,' Reg said as he clicked the seatbelt.

'Good morning, Reg. You're looking very swish today,' she said.

Reg looked down at his suit and brushed his hands over the shiny suit trousers. 'Long time since I've been to the big smoke.'

'The big smoke? Are you flying to Brisbane?'

He chuckled, and as she glanced over Callie noticed he'd even shaved this morning.

'No, down to Charleville, love. I don't think I've been down there for a couple of years.'

Callie put the indicator on, shifted the sports car into gear, and pulled out into the main street. It was quite busy this morning. Sue Watts had a cake stall near the butcher's shop, and a group of Augathella Primary School kids were walking to the library. They certainly hadn't taken much time to get the kids out and about.

She kept a close eye on the group because it was Nigel's class and frowned when she didn't spot him.

'What are you looking so worried about?' Reg asked.

'I think that's Nigel's class, but I can't seem to spot him.'

Reg turned to look and said, 'Yeah, there he is, love. He's bringing up the rear with the teacher. They're still waiting to cross the road.'

As they drove, they took the southern exit out of town and turned right onto the Matilda

Highway. Callie glanced across at Reg again.

'I could've picked you up at your house,' she said.

Reg's voice was gruff. 'You know where I live, do you?'

'Braden told me the other day. I could have saved you a walk.'

'No,' he said. 'I had to go into town and have a haircut and a shave. The barber's got to make a living. Seems there aren't many blokes in town who go to him anymore. All the young blokes these days go to the hairdresser. Talk about pansies.'

Callie made a non-committal noise.

'What about Braden? Where does he get his hair cut?' Reg persisted with the thread of conversation.

She felt guilty. 'I cut it for him. He finds it hard to get into town. He's so busy at the moment.'

'That's fair enough, love,' Reg said.

They drove on, and Callie tried not to look at the house on the right as they cruised down the hill.

'You can look if you want to,' he said.

'I didn't want to seem to be a stickybeak,' she said.

Reg looked sad as he stared ahead.

Chapter 8

'We're like Thelma and Louise,' Alana said with a grin as they exited the ramp onto the westbound highway. Jenna had had an early appointment at the local solicitor's office. Alana had come in and waited in the foyer. 'Thelma and Louise who?' Jenna asked.

'That's right, I forgot you don't watch movies.'

'Oh, I think I've heard about it. Didn't they both die in the end? That's not how I want to start this trip, hearing stuff like that.'

'No, it's a new adventure,' she said. 'Maybe we'll meet Brad Pitt on the way.'

'I told you the other day I don't need a man in my life.'

Alana shook her head and wagged her finger at Jenna. 'Famous last words, love. Famous last words.'

'No, I'm putting all of my energy into my new business.' She flashed a grin at Alana. 'Our new business. I'm so pleased you've come in with me. It's going to make such a difference having someone to help me.'

'How much "doing up" is there for us to do? I can wield a paintbrush.'

'The photos of it don't look too bad. It's an old place. I think maybe a coat of paint and some new furniture. It shouldn't take us too long.'

'And have you applied for all the proper permits to run a business out there where it is?'

Jenna nodded. 'I have. I've got all the necessary certificates and permits from the local shire. The only funny thing was that the guy at the council said he'll have to send the building inspector up after we do it all up. I didn't think a building inspector would want to see that a place had been painted.'

'Sounds a bit strange. Are you sure the photos were okay?'

'Yeah, it looked spacious. I've got the floor plan too. As well as the coffee machine, I'll need to buy a couple of new appliances for the kitchen, probably a dishwasher and maybe a new stove. We'll see what the other ones are like. And some appliances.'

'And you've got a unit for us to live in while we're doing the place up? Did you need to?'

'Yeah, a unit came up. I thought it was wise just in case the place needed more work than I thought, and when the agent told me about this unit, I agreed to take a three-month lease. One of the primary school teachers has moved to

Brisbane; there are two bedrooms, and the rent's not too bad. I think I told you what it was the other day, didn't I?'

'Yep, all good. Now we've got to sort out how I'm going to be doing this business with you.'

Jenna nodded. 'I thought we'd agreed that I'll pay you a wage.'

'Have you ever thought about me putting some money in and going into the business with you?' Alana sounded hesitant.

Jenna preferred to go it alone, but didn't want to hurt her friend's feelings or have her think that she might have thought Alana was unreliable. Which, she had to admit to herself, Alana didn't have a good track record with any job.

'Don't take it the wrong way, but I have to go into this by myself; it was a condition of the loan from the bank. Don't worry, I'll pay you well, the going rate plus ten percent.'

Alana laughed. 'That's not what I meant. I just thought it'd be nice to have a finger in the pie, so to speak.'

'You will. You'll be baking the pies.'

'I'm looking forward to it,' Alana said with a chuckle. 'I love the sound of a vintage tea room.'

Relief filled Jenna; she hadn't wanted to put Alana offside. 'Did I tell you I went to the op shop at Southport the other day, and I got the best clothes? And when I got my hair trimmed before we decided when to leave, my hairdresser showed me how to do that 1940s tight roll.'

Alana nodded. 'And you should see the absolutely gorgeous red lipstick I've got. We're gonna slay them in the aisles, kiddo.'

'I can't wait. I've got all Gran's recipes. I've been practising baking scones, and I reckon this is going to be fantastic. And we're coming into the green season. The highway should be busy. Who knows, we might make a fortune in the first month.'

The three days of travel passed quickly, and they spent their last night in Charleville, hoping they could get an early start the next morning for the very short trip up the highway to Augathella. While they were there, they had a look at the World War II airbase, and Jenna had a chat with the lady at the counter about their new venture up the highway.

'Sounds great,' the woman said. 'If you get some advertising material done, I'd be happy to put up flyers here in the cabinet. We get lots of tourists coming through in the winter—actually all year—but winter is when the grey nomads hit the highway. And if you get flyers done, make sure you put them in the tourist information centre and the caravan parks.'

Jenna nodded. 'Yes, my mum and dad have been travelling like that for about ten years, and I know how many people they meet on the road and what they like. So, fingers crossed, we're hoping it will be a success.'

'I think it's a great idea,' the woman said.

After dinner at the Corones Hotel and the luxury of staying overnight in one of the fabulous suites there, the next morning Jenna and Alana picked up the keys to the unit in Augathella as soon as Jenna had finished at the solicitor's office.

Even though it was winter, the sun promised a warm day. As they drove out of Charleville just before eleven, mist still lingered in the paddocks, creating an eerie image as black cattle loomed out of the trees.

'It's certainly different from what I imagined,' Alana said. 'I thought it would be the outback with red dirt and dust. I must say

I'm a little bit surprised.'

'It really is quite a pretty place. Look at the silvery leaves on those trees.'

'Do you think you'll stay out here long?' Alana asked.

Jenna shrugged. 'Well, I want to find somewhere new to live. There's nothing for me on the coast anymore, and I've got to hate how crowded it was. Mum and Dad are on the road, so I'm sure I'll see them every year or so as they come through. What about you?'

'I'll probably stay for a year, maybe longer. If you're happy to have me, you might need a whole heap more staff if this takes off.'

Jenna grinned at her friend. 'But it would be nice. If I do, you can be the manager of the floor.'

'What did you think of all those photos of the 1940s clothes we saw in the museum at Charleville? I can't wait to see what you bought.'

Jenna glanced at her watch. 'Settlement is at one o'clock. It's almost mine.'

'It was a good idea of yours, getting a local solicitor to do all the stuff for you and having it settled as soon as we arrived. He seemed like a nice guy when he came out of his office with you.'

'He was pretty cute, actually.'

'I didn't think you were interested in dating?'

'I'm out here to work. It doesn't hurt to look at the local scenery, though. He seemed a bit surprised that two city girls were coming out to Augathella to start a new business. He asked me if I'd seen the house yet, and when I said no, he frowned. And then he asked me if I'd ever been to Augathella, and when I said no, he looked shocked.'

'The receptionist chatted to me a bit while I

was waiting for you. She asked me if I knew what a small town Augathella was, and I said we're not targeting the town.'

'Although, if we get a good reputation, we might find a lot of the locals will come in for coffee.'

'Jenna, did you see that beautiful girl walking through the foyer when we walked in?'

'Yes, I did. She was really pretty. She looked familiar to me, but I don't know anyone out this way.'

'And she was very friendly. Lovely smile she gave us. I do like country folk.'

'Country folk, Alana? It's starting to sound like you're a yokel yourself.'

'A local yokel, that's what I'll be,' Alana said with a grin.

Jenna glanced at the navigation screen, and her excitement rose. 'We're only ten kilometres out of Augathella, and the place is two kilometres south of the turnoff. So, keep your eye out another eight kilometres, and you should see a little cottage on the left.'

'Is it going to be out here by itself?' Alana asked. 'I haven't seen any other houses since we left Charleville. Just the occasional farmhouse set back from the road. Is it just on a normal suburban block?'

'No, it's on an acre. I've even been thinking that once we get the inside of the place done and the business up and going, we can start doing some garden settings, maybe have some little grottos and things like that.'

'You're full of plans,' Alana said as she kept her eyes to the left.

'I am. I'm really excited about this.'

'Are you going to be able to afford it all?'

'I am. My gran left me quite a nice little sum. But I still have to be careful and make sure I get a good return on investment. I've got to work out prices and what it'll cost me to bake everything.'

'And milk and tea and coffee, and crockery and stuff.'

'Did you see that big timber crate in the back underneath our suitcases?'

Alana nodded. 'I thought that was a toolbox.'

'No.' Jenna shook her head. 'It's full of my Gran's collectible china. That's what gave me the idea in the first place. She used to love her tea in a Shelley teacup, and it was a real treat for me when I was little. Mum and Dad used to take us around to Gran's place in Morningside, and she would always have a high tea ready for us. She used to make me go and wash my face and hands when I'd been playing outside with the neighbour's kids. I had to comb my hair and take my shorts and T-shirt off and put on a pretty dress. Then we'd sit up at her high dining room table and have a high tea. The pouring of the tea was a ritual.'

'Sounds like fun,' Alana said. 'The most my grandparents ever did was send me to the shops to buy milk. Although I did get a couple of dollars for lollies.'

'I miss Gran so much.'

'What about your grandfather?'

'Never had one. Gran was a single mum, and she brought Mum up by herself. It was a really big thing to have a child out of wedlock in those days, as Mum used to call it, but Gran was always happy.'

'Was her boyfriend killed in the war?'

'I don't know what happened to him. Gran was always very quiet about that. It's a family mystery.'

'Maybe you could do the genetic stuff with the DNA tests and all that. What do they call it? Ancestry.com?'

'I'm not really interested,' Jenna said. 'I don't know what happened to him, and I doubt if he'd be alive anymore.'

'What about your mum?'

'Mum was always quite closed about it. I think it bothered her, not having a dad when she grew up.'

'Two kilometres to go,' Alana said, looking at the Google map on her phone. 'Maybe go a little bit slower so I can spot it.'

A small hill appeared on the left, and as they began to climb, Alana rolled her eyes. 'Gosh, I hope it doesn't look like that place.'

An overgrown paddock with falling-down fences met their eyes about fifty metres back from the road. A rutted dirt driveway led to an old, tumbledown cottage that sat on the crest of the hill. Even with the bright morning sun, it looked dark and uninviting. A crooked milk can was painted with the number RMB 182.

'I hope seeing that place doesn't turn the tourists off when they see it before they get to our place.'

Jenna kept driving slowly, and they travelled another three kilometres.

'There are no more houses on the left,' Alana said. 'Does your house have a number?'

'I don't know. It's before the turnoff, and we passed that about two kilometres ago. I'm sure he said south of town. Maybe I misheard the instructions. Maybe it's north of the turnoff.' Jenna pulled over and parked on the side of the road. She reached for her bag on the back seat and pulled out the paperwork the solicitor had given her.

'It's RMB 182.'

They looked at each other.

'It can't be that place,' Alana said quietly.

'No, it won't be. It's nothing like the photos in the ad. I'll do a U-turn, and we'll go back and have a look.'

'Where's your phone? Can I open it and have a look at the ad?'

Jenna pointed to the console behind the gearshift, and Alana reached for her phone. 'What's the password?'

'It's my birthday,' Jenna said.

'That's not very secure.'

'Doesn't matter. There's nothing private on the phone. The ad's in the photos. It's about two weeks old.'

Jenna scrolled through Alana's phone and paused and stared at the screen. She turned to Alana as the old cottage on the hill appeared ahead of them. Alana looked at the phone again and then glanced across at Jenna.

'RMB 182,' she said.

Jenna widened her eyes as she slowed right down and stared at the cottage on the hill.

'Oh my God, Alana, what have I done?'

Chapter 9

Callie walked out of the obstetrician's office, feeling comfortable and relaxed. The doctor had reassured her that everything was on track. The baby was growing well, and his or her heartbeat was strong and steady. Her blood pressure was spot on, and all of the other tests that he had run had come back satisfactory. The only thing that he'd commented on was the size of the baby and he had booked her in for a scan at next week's visit.

She walked across to the pub opposite where she'd parked her car near the town hall. The street was busy today, and she had to wait while caravans drove past, heading out towards the World War II Centre. Reg was sitting in the sun with an empty beer glass in front of him. His appointment with the solicitor had been a little bit earlier than her doctor's appointment. She'd waited with him in the office until he went in, and then went to see the doctor in the same building. Callie knew if he came out first, he'd have a beer while he waited for her.

'How did it go, Reg?' she asked. 'All done?'

'I am. I even got my bit of shopping done.' He pointed to a plastic bag on the floor beside him. 'So, did the doc say you're still allowed to drive that flash sports car home?'

'I surely am. Unless you want to drive?' she said.

He harrumphed. 'Me? I haven't driven for years.'

Callie was determined to find out something about Reg's past, so she looked at him with her

84

head tilted to the side. 'Would you like to grab an early lunch before we head back?'

'Your shout, love,' he said, his grin cheeky. 'Maybe we could have an early bite to eat. I think I could stretch to a sandwich and a cup of tea. Does that suit you, lass?'

'It does. I'm starving,' she replied.

They walked along the street and found a new coffee shop around the corner, near the council chambers. Callie ordered a salami baguette while Reg went for the roast beef and pickle sandwich. She knew she would regret it later, but she was starving and hadn't had a gourmet baguette since she left Brisbane two years ago. When they'd been there with Petie a few months back, they'd lived on plastic-wrapped sandwiches from the hospital café.

As they waited for the meals to be brought to the table, she looked at Reg. 'I've known you for well over eighteen months now, and I'm curious. Tell me, how long have you lived in Augathella?'

He stared at her steadily. 'I've lived in Augathella for over sixty years.'

'So, you weren't born here?' she asked, but he remained silent for a few minutes.

'I went away, and I got on the shearing circuit when I was a young lad. Then I came back to town,' he finally replied.

'And what did you do when you came back to town?'

'I drove a truck for quite a few years. I used to actually take stuff out to Braden's place when his parents were still alive. He was just a young whippersnapper. He probably wouldn't remember.'

'He's never mentioned it, so he probably doesn't,' she said.

The young waitress put their sandwiches on the table, and they thanked her. 'So, Reg, you've always been a loner. You've never had a wife or a family?'

He tapped his finger on the side of his nose. 'That would be telling, wouldn't it?'

Her curiosity was piqued. 'Oh, so you've never had a wife?'

He sighed. 'I never took myself a wife. There was someone once, a long, long time ago who I would have married.'

'What happened, Reg?'

'One day when we've got a lot of time, I'll tell you, love. But for now, we've got lunch, and then we've got an hour's drive back home.'

'I'm not being a stickybeak. I sometimes worry about you being lonely.'

'Me lonely? I'm not lonely, love, and I'll be less lonely from next week.'

'Next week. Is that why you went to the solicitors?' she asked.

'I've sold my house, love. I'm moving into

the aged care home in town.'

'Wow, that's a big move.'

'I figured I might as well get someone to cook meals for me and someone to have a yarn with, and it's a lot less distance to walk to the pub every day.'

Callie grinned. 'It sure is. Who bought your house?'

'Some girl from Brisbane. Don't know why she'd want to come and move out here,' he said apologetically.

'I did.'

'But you had a reason too, didn't you?'

'Best move, best decision I ever made in my whole life,' she said. 'So, when do you move into town?'

'Well, I can move in any time now that we've signed on the bottom line. Apparently, this woman is coming in the next few days, and she just has to come into the solicitors and sign.

It's all organised. I'll have the money this afternoon at one o'clock, I can pay the home fees, and I can move into my new room when it's all sorted.' Reg looked down at the big old gold watch on his wrist. 'Actually, that's only an hour away. Maybe we could go via the bank on the way out.'

'Of course, we can. We have plenty of time. I don't have to be back until school comes out.'

'Thank you, love.'

Callie sat back and put her hands on her stomach. She could feel the effects of that salami already. 'Well, that's certainly big news.' She picked up her cup of tea. 'Now, we have time. Tell me about this person that you loved once.'

'Oh, it's not much of a story, love. I met Meggie back in the sixties. We spent some time together, and she decided I wasn't good enough for her family. I was a shearer back then. I'd planned to marry her, but it wasn't meant to be. I was heartbroken, a bit lonely for a while, but I learned to live with it.' When Reg's eyes met Callie's, they were sad. 'I never got over her, ya know. There's not a day goes by when I don't think about her. Wonder where she is, whether she had a happy life, that sort of thing.'

Callie blinked to clear the moisture from her eyes. She reached over the table and held Reg's hand. 'Would you like to talk about her?'

For a moment he hesitated and she thought she might have overstepped the mark.

'That's the first time I've said her name for many years.' Reg's voice was a bit husky and he cleared his throat. 'You're a good girl, Callie. You care about people, not just what they can do for you. I see so many types in the pub every day, and I'm a pretty damn good judge of character and let me tell you, Braden Cartwright was damn lucky when you put your bags in that drain.'

'How on earth did you know about that?' she exclaimed. 'Braden promised he wouldn't tell anyone.'

'But did the boys promise?' Reg's thin shoulders shook underneath the shiny suit jacket as he laughed.

She was pleased to see the sadness had gone from his eyes.

'I know everything that happens within a hundred miles of Augathella.'

Callie grinned back at him. 'So, tell me about your Meggie and what happened a long time ago.'

'She was the prettiest girl I ever laid eyes on. She was working at the local bakery. I was shearing out on the remote stations in the sixties, and I didn't see many girls, but she stopped me in my tracks that day I went in to buy a pie.

'Back then they used to have dances in the hall on Saturday nights, and after I went in there three days in a row to buy a pie—just so I could look at her—I got up the courage to ask her out.'

'And?' Callie prompted.

'And I've never eaten so many pies in my life.'

'No, I meant what did she say?'

'She said yes. We went to lots of dances whenever I was close by, and then I got a job driving trucks with Horrie, Jim Andersen's dad, so I could stay in town. We used to go for picnics on the river, and we saw a lot of each other in those six months.'

'What happened?'

'One month I had a big trip to do for Horrie, and when I came back after three weeks away, she was gone.'

'Gone? Do you know why? Or where?'

Reg slipped his hand into his jacket and pulled out his wallet. His hands shook as he pulled out a piece of paper. The paper was so flimsy it was almost transparent. 'I'll let you read it, as long as you don't tell a soul. Not even Braden.' He held it out to Callie and looked away from her as she took it.

'If you're sure, Reg?'

'I am. You've been kind to me, Callie.'

The writing was loopy and the ink was faded, but Callie could easily read the words. She glanced across at Reg, but he was looking away from her, his lips were pressed together, and she would swear he had tears in his eyes. As she swallowed, the baby gave a ferocious kick, first on one side of her ribs and then there was a big roll, and then a kick on the opposite side. Maybe Braden was right, and it was a boy.

She put one hand on her stomach, but the kicking eased as she began to read.

Dearest Reg,

I know I'm a coward but I couldn't tell you this to your face. I'm moving to Brisbane. Augathella is not enough for me. I want more out of life. I don't want to live in the bush, and I know how much you love it. I want a house in the city. Where it rains and where flowers will grow all year. I want a life where I can go to the pictures, and go shopping when I want to. Not have to wait until there is a bus to Charleville. The bush feeds your soul as you told me so romantically that night we lay under the stars. I will never forget that night and I will never forget you.

Thank you for the loveliest six months of my life. You are a very lovely man. I wish you a happy and successful life.

Warmest regards
Margaret Hope

Callie blinked back tears as she carefully folded the letter and passed it back to Reg. She sensed that he didn't want to say any more so she looked down at the half-eaten baguette and pushed her plate towards him.

'I can't eat the rest of this. Would you like the rest of my sandwich?'

'With that wog food on it? Not bloody likely, lassie. Give me roast beef and pickles any day,' he replied, his voice still a bit shaky despite his gruff words.

'Do you want another cup of tea?'

'No, let's go home.'

Chapter 10

Jenna and Alana stood on the front porch of the ramshackle cottage looking over the long grass and the gardens full of weeds. Two large chimneys flanked the eastern side, and a brick outside toilet was on the other side.

Alana looked at Jenna. 'How much did you say you paid for this place?'

'Not much,' Jenna replied slowly. 'No wonder it was so cheap and now I know why the solicitor guy was looking doubtful.'

'Look on the bright side.' Alana spread her arms wide.

'Is there one?' Jenna kicked at the rotten

floor boards on the veranda where they stood.

'There is!' Alana's eyes were shining. 'I love a challenge, don't you? That's what's been missing in my life for so long. Working for greedy people who just want to make money. You've got a dream and you want to create something special here. And look!' Alana pointed to the road. Caravan after caravan passed by, pulled by large four-wheel drive vehicles heading north.

A surge of enthusiasm raced through Jenna as she counted seven caravans going past. 'Look at them all!'

'And not one of them turned into Augathella,' Alana said.

'They are my market. We have to get working, and tidying, and cleaning and scrubbing.'

'We do.' Alana carefully stepped across the broken floorboard. 'It's the beginning of the tourist season. We can have this place up and running by the time they all head back south to wherever they come from.'

'We can! Let's be positive. What's it really going to take besides some timber and paint and a lot of hard work. Are you sure you want to put that much work in, Alana?'

Alana looked at the holes in the front door and the three-legged chair. 'It's gonna take a hell of a lot of work, but count me in.' She laughed. 'And we haven't even seen inside yet!'

'You really think we can do it? Close your eyes and imagine. Imagine a big circular driveway coming in over there.' Jenna pointed to the front yard. 'With lots of space to park caravans. And even buses.'

'You've got a good imagination. It could be a circle, but it's full of potholes, red dirt, long grass, and lumps of rock. A little bit of elbow grease on a mower and yes, we can fix it.'

'I'll have to buy a ride-on mower with an acre.'

'According to Google there's a hardware store in Augathella, and we can go get some new timber and make a new floor. Come on, let's go and look inside. Are you really sure you want to stay?'

'I am. Are we supposed to go inside before it's yours?'

'I signed the final papers this morning at the solicitors, and my money is going over at one o'clock.' Jenna pulled out her phone and checked the time. 'I'm sure no one is going to complain about me being here fifteen minutes before it becomes mine. Just don't fall through the floorboards until after one.'

Alana laughed. 'You do have insurance?'

'I do and I took out public liability for the business as well.'

Alana shook her head slowly from side to

side. 'I don't believe we're here. Give us a month, and you won't recognise this place.'

'I'm really excited about it,' Jenna followed Alana to the front door. She'd expected her friend to be horrified when they'd pulled up and realised that this old, falling-down shack was what she'd bought. But as she watched the caravans and cars on the highway, she knew that when she fixed it up, she could make a success of it.

I will.

'Look, here's my first customer now,' Jenna said, her eyes lighting up as a red sports car turned off the road and into the overgrown driveway.

'It can't be your first customer. We're not ready, and it's not legally yours yet,' Alana protested.

'Close enough.' Jenna widened her eyes as she recognised the pretty woman she had seen in the solicitor's office. The elderly guy was helping her out of the sports car. 'That's the lady we saw in Charleville.'

'I wonder what they're doing,' Alana said.

The pair walked across the end of the driveway and up the two steps onto the veranda. The woman was smiling, but she kept shooting worried glances at the old man walking beside her.

'Hello,' Jenna called out. 'How can I help you? I can't help with any directions, I'm sorry. We've just arrived here.'

The old man looked up at her and grabbed the rickety stair rail. His face went white, and his mouth opened and closed as he stared up at her.

The woman with him grabbed his arm. 'Reg, are you okay? What's wrong?'

The man stared at Jenna, his eyes huge and one hand on his chest. She worried that he was having a heart attack or a turn of some kind. He looked quite old. He lifted his hand to his throat, and for a moment, she thought he was going to pass out and fall to the ground. 'Would you like to come up and sit down?' she offered. 'There's a chair here.'

'I know there's a bloody chair there. It's my chair, at least it will be for another ten minutes,' Jenna realised at the same time as Alana looked at her, wide-eyed.

'Are you Mr. MacGilvray? Are you the owner?' Jenna asked. The man was still pale.

'I am. Who are you?' he asked, still looking at her with wide eyes and an open mouth.

Chapter 11

Callie was worried that Reg was having some sort of episode; she had never seen him so pale and shaky. He hadn't taken his eyes off the two young women above them on the front veranda.

'Reg, what do you want to do? Do you want to go back to the pub or stay here?' she asked. Then she looked at the two young women. 'You've just stopped in here to see the place, right?' she asked hesitantly. 'Or did you come to see Reg?'

'I don't know them,' Reg said. A little bit of colour had come back into his face but he was

103

still staring at the young woman with the long, dark, curly hair.

'No, we've just stopped to have a look for now. I've actually bought this place,' the taller woman said.

'Oh, you're the new owners. Reg told me he's sold it.' Callie thought about what a pretty young woman she was, but she still kept shooting worried glances at Reg. He was sitting on the chair now, his arms dangling between his legs, looking at the rot in the floorboards. Perhaps he felt guilty about the state the house was in.

He lifted his head. 'You can stay here. I'll just grab my gear and I'll stay at the pub tonight if you want to move in.'

'Oh, there's no need to do that, Mr MacGilvray. We're staying in town for a couple of months. We've actually rented a place there.'

'We haven't made any introductions. I'm

Callie Cartwright, and I live about thirty kilometres out of town. I just gave Reg a lift down to Charleville this morning.'

'I'm Jenna Wilson,' the tall woman said.

'And I'm Alana Rickman,' the other woman said. 'I've come out to help my friend Jenna with her new venture.'

'Your new venture?' Callie asked, her eyebrows raised.

'Yes, we're turning this into a cafe.'

'A bloody cafe! You gotta be bloody joking,' Reg burst out, and Callie tried to catch his eye.

'I think that sounds like a wonderful idea,' Callie turned to the two young women. 'Welcome to town. You'll love living in Augathella. It's the best place to live and work. Where have you come from?'

'We spent the last three days driving from Brisbane.'

Callie chuckled. 'As I did two years ago.' She sensed the girls' eyes on her pregnant stomach. 'I met somebody here, and I live here now. And we're about to have our first baby. That'll make it four.' Callie smiled when the young women frowned.

'You've been here two years, and you've got four children?' Jenna asked.

'I have three stepsons, and this is our first baby together. My husband and I, that is.'

'Enough of that,' Reg interrupted. 'Come on, I'll soon find out enough about this idea.'

'Please don't rush. We can go. We just called to have a quick look at the place. Don't let us impose,' Jenna said. She and her friend turned towards the steps. 'It was good to meet you. I'm sure we'll catch up.'

'We're going into town as well. Are you sure you want to come in to town, Reg?'

'Well, it'll save me the bloody walk. And it

means I won't have to carry my gear.'

'Please Mr MacGilvray, you don't have to do it this afternoon. There's no rush.'

'I'll do it now,' he said. 'It won't take long.'

'Do you want me to help you pack anything?' Callie noticed that Reg was looking anywhere except at the woman called Jenna.

***

Jenna looked at Mr MacGilvray when he walked out of the house with a bag over one shoulder and a small box in his hand. He put the bag on the floor and then placed the box carefully on the chair near the rotten floorboards.

A small clock and a fine china tea cup rested on a stained tea towel. The way he placed the box gently on the chair it was as though it held a whole lifetime's worth of his precious things.

'Come on, Callie, it's time we got going. You take this bag and the box and I'll go back for my suitcase.' He went back into the house. Jenna felt as though they were intruding in his last time in his home.

'Can I help?' Jenna offered, meeting Callie's eyes. She looked sad too.

'Thank you. Perhaps if you take the small bag and the box,' Callie said. 'I'd like to have two hands to hang on going down the steps.'

'When are you due?' Jenna asked as she reached down to pick up the box.

'Four weeks.'

Jenna stared at her and a niggle of memory tugged. 'I feel as though I know you. What did you do in Brisbane?'

Callie's cheeks reddened. 'I . . .um . . .worked in weather.'

Jenna smiled. 'You were that wonderful weather girl in the clip that went viral. I knew I recognised your face in the solicitor's office.'

Callie nodded and her smile was rueful. 'I

don't know if I'd say wonderful.'

'You were.' Jenna followed her down the steps to the red sports car. 'And you moved from the city to here and you love it? That encourages me. I've been having doubts about the move already.'

'Don't,' Callie said. 'It's the most wonderful community. I've made so many friends and our social calendar is always full. My husband' — she smiled '—I still can't get quite used to saying that, is busy with the cattle muster at the moment, otherwise I'd invite you out to *Kilcoy Station*. There are many young people in the district now and since the drought broke, there's been a huge influx of young couples.'

'It sounds good.'

'We usually come into the pub for dinner once a fortnight or so. They do good meals, and you'll meet lots of locals there.'

Alana had followed them down the steps.

'Only couples? Are there many single guys around?'

Callie's smile widened. 'A few. There's a get-together to welcome the new arrivals in town in a couple of weeks. I'll get the details to you when I know when it's on. Where are you staying?'

When Jenna told her the address of the unit, Callie nodded.

'That's Jacinta's apartment. She's moved back to Brisbane. So, would you like to come to the get-together?'

'Sounds good,' Jenna said.

Callie looked up and Jenna turned to follow her gaze. 'Here's Reg now.'

'Where's he moving to?'

'He's going into aged care,' Callie whispered.

Reg clomped down the steps. 'I've got all my gear. Look after the old place, girl. She's been good to me.' Before Jenna could answer, he hoisted a suitcase into the small back seat of the car, and held the door open for Callie as she climbed in awkwardly. He got into the passenger street and didn't look up again.

'See you both later. Good luck,' Callie said as she started the engine. 'And if you need anything just ask in town. Someone will help you.'

Jenna and Alana watched as the cute little red car turned onto the highway.

'That was interesting,' Alana said.

'It was. I felt sad for him, and mean that we were in his house.'

'He didn't have much, did he?'

'Maybe he'd moved it earlier and that was the last of it.'

'I hope so. Come on. Let's go and see what I've bought, and see how much work we've got ahead.'

Chapter 12

'Did you see the way that Reg guy looked at you, Jen?' Alana asked as they drove into town.

'I did. He made me feel really uncomfortable. I thought he was going to pass out there for a while. Maybe he was upset to see someone had actually bought his house.'

'He must've been in the solicitor's office when we passed Callie in the foyer. Wasn't she lovely?'

'She was. The solicitor didn't mention that the vendor was there before me. I didn't notice him come out of the office though, did you?'

'No, I didn't.'

'Callie was very welcoming. It was lovely of her to invite us to that get-together she mentioned. Will we go, Alana?'

'Of course.'

'I didn't think I'd be able to keep you away.' Jenna nudged her. 'An opportunity to scope out the local talent.'

'You've got me interested.' Alana smiled. Seriously though, can I ask you one thing, Jen? I'm a bit curious. Especially now that we've seen this place. Why did you choose it? Surely you could've got something better way closer to the city?'

Jenna glanced across at Alana. 'The first reason was, it was really cheap. Really, really cheap. It fit all my requirements. On the highway, close to a town, and on some land but I guess I should've known that it was going to need a lot of work. I was in real estate, for goodness' sake! I think it was the other reason that I wanted to come this far out that put blinkers on my reasoning.'

'The other reason?' Alana asked curiously.

'I wanted to come out here because this is where Gran grew up.' When she talked about the place her face lit up.

'What about your mum? Did she grow up here too?'

'No, Gran left here when she was in her teens. I often wondered why she stayed in Brisbane, but I guess it was to give Mum the chance of a good education, and more opportunities as she grew up.'

'When she passed, I invested what she left me, and I vowed I'd come out here one day and check out where she grew up. When the cottage came on the market, I thought there was no better way to spend her inheritance than to come out where Gran grew up.'

'It's funny, you know, this landscape really

appeals to me. It's very different to the coastal landscape, but I like it,' Alana said.

'It is. Anyway, let's head into town and hope that where we're staying is a little bit more upmarket than my cottage. The fourth street on the left is Nelson Street. Then on the right, the agent said we'll see three brick units and a large carport.'

'I'll tell you when to turn.'

As they drove along the old Charleville Road, Jenna was thoughtful. She felt guilty that she'd bought the house from old Mr MacGilvray. He'd looked absolutely stricken to see that there were actually new owners, and she knew that the amount of money that she paid for it would barely fund his retirement.

Maybe after a couple of days, she'd go and visit him and check he was okay.

***

Callie was sad, but she tried to hide it from

Reg. Seeing the old house he'd lived in and his few belongings had really shocked her. But it was his reaction to the new owner that had worried her; she'd even considered calling the ambulance for a few minutes until the colour had come back to his face.

It must have been the realisation that he was leaving the house that he'd lived in for many years. She was glad that they were close to town.

'So, where should I drop you off?' she asked as they passed the rural store. 'Do you want me to drop you at the . . . at your new home . . . or take you straight to the pub?'

'The pub. I'll sleep there until my room is ready next week.'

'What about your stuff?'

'It can stay with me. I've already brought the rest of my things. I carried a bit when I walked in each day. Sean let me put it all in the back storeroom at the pub.'

Callie wondered about the contents of the box. The small clock was ornate, and the teacup looked like a Shelley vintage cup. Her heart broke. Reg had walked the five kilometres every day with some of his belongings. Why didn't anyone in town know what he was doing and that he needed help? She promised herself she'd go and see Maisie Ramsay at the home and check he had everything he needed. If he didn't, she'd buy what he needed next time she went to Charleville. It was time someone looked out for him.

'This was just the last of it that I needed last night,' he said.

'Are you feeling okay now?' she asked carefully.

'I am,' he said.

'I might come in with you and have a cold drink.'

'Suit yourself.'

'I will. I've got plenty of time. We can keep yarning.'

Reg was such a strange fellow. Who knew what was going through his mind? Everything seemed guarded, but he didn't reveal much about himself. He knew everything there was to know about Augathella, the history and settlement, the families and who belonged where, but who knew anything about him? Even Braden who'd known him all his life knew little.

Sure, he had opened up to her today but now he was closed as tight as a clam shell.

She turned right at Biddenham Street and drove around the back of the pub and parked there. The car could stay there until Braden or Fallon came into town at three. She glanced down at her watch. It was just after two, another hour and school would be out.

'Do you mind if I come in and have a lemon squash with you?' she asked.

Reg shrugged. 'Suit yourself.'

This closed-down man was totally out of character for the usual friendly Reg. He'd gone inside himself when he'd seen Jenna and Alana on the veranda of his house. For a moment, he looked as though he had seen a ghost. His eyes widened, and then his mouth dropped open in shock. Callie suspected it had more to do with her, rather than her being the new owner of his house. She was going to get to the bottom of this even if it took all afternoon.

'I'm going to have to ask you a favour again,' she said, pulling a face as he climbed out of the passenger seat of the low-slung sports car.

'Yes,' he said, turning to face her.

'Can you come around and help me get out of the car again, please?'

His face softened, and the old Reg resurfaced as he walked around the back of the car and opened her door.

He smiled as he held out both hands 'Sorry, I've been a bit cranky, love.'

His skin was rough and papery but his grip was surprisingly firm. He held her elbow firmly as she pushed herself up to her feet. 'Thank you, Reg. You're a true gentleman. And strong!'

'Now, let me buy you a beer for driving me all the way down to Charleville.' Her stomach gurgled.

'Are you hungry, lass?' He laughed and Callie relaxed as he held her elbow as they walked into the pub together.

'Actually, I am, but I know they won't be serving this time of the day. I'll see if Sean's around. He might have a bowl of fruit salad or something in the cool room. If not, I'll have a bag of chips.' She chuckled. 'I've given up worrying about my weight.'

'Damn,' Reg said. 'I forgot my box.' He led Callie over to his usual table. 'You sit here while I get it, and when I come back, I'll find Sean.' He made sure she was settled comfortably.

'Thank you. Like I said before, Reg, you're a true gentleman.' Callie leaned back in the chair and looked along the street. There was not a soul to be seen, and the coffee shop down the road had already closed for the day. Someone came out of the butcher's as she watched, and a sole caravan rumbled slowly down the road, heading towards the free camp near the river.

It was a peaceful country scene after all the rain. The footpath in the park was green, the sky was a brilliant blue, and she put her head back and closed her eyes. The warm afternoon sun relaxed her.

She must've drifted off briefly. When she opened her eyes again, Reg was sitting there, staring into the distance. A glass of lemon squash was on a coaster in front of her, and a bowl of fruit salad with a fork and spoon sat on a place mat in front of her.

'You're an absolute gem, Reg. Thank you so much,' she said, fighting back tears. 'I just caught forty winks. I'll be glad when this baby's born. I've never needed so much sleep in the afternoon.'

'You were snoring.'

'I was not,' Callie said indignantly. 'Ladies don't snore.'

'It was a pretty little snore. Not like old Jim Andersen when he nods off at the bar. You can hear him from out here.' Reg laughed and Callie smiled. He'd come right out of his mood.

'Won't hurt you. I like my little naps out here. And this is the time to have it, between two and three in the afternoon. The town's dead until school comes out. Then all the mums and school buses break the peace and quiet and soon after that, all the local cockies come in for their beer, and the fun begins.'

'The town does come alive then.'

'Best time of day in the pub. Did I tell you what I heard last week?' he said.

'You might have. You've told me a lot about what happens here, Reg,' Callie said. She glanced down and noticed the box on the third chair on the other side of Reg.

Reg lifted his middy of beer, took a deep draft, and Callie smiled. Froth stuck to his whiskers.

'Craig Wilson was in here, and apparently, he and Mandy had a blue before he left home. Something to do with their young bloke, Rusty.'

Callie shook her head. Reg's knowledge of the local community amazed her.

'Never did find out the upshot of what it was all about. Rusty came in to pick him up and told him that a bunch of flowers would do the trick at home. Jim Andersen told him there was some pretty stuff that had just come up behind his garage, so Craig went and picked a big bunch of it. And then he took a whole bunch of flowers home.'

'Oh, that was nice of him. It would have cheered Mandy up.'

Reg started cackling. 'It was bloody lantana. A noxious weed. It's only just appeared out here in the west and he thought it was a flower. After Craig left, Jim had us all falling about laughing.'

Callie laughed, and after a while, Reg's shoulders shook as he laughed silently.

'Apparently, she threw them out and he got the dirts with her until Rusty told him he'd picked her a bunch of weeds. He brought

Mandy in here for dinner the next night.'

Callie shook her head. 'You don't miss a trick, Reg.'

'You know what, love? I'll be glad to be in town all the time,' he said. 'Doesn't matter about that old house. Just a house, isn't it, love? Bits of timber, bits of dirt, it'll be there long after I'm gone.'

Callie chose her words carefully. 'It will be nice to see it renovated a little bit, and I think the idea that those girls have got sounds like a plan. Sometimes it can be hard to get a coffee in town, and the caravans soon hear that and keep going on the highway. If they see the new cafe, they come into town and stay. We might get some more people in town. It's always good for business, isn't it, Reg?'

He dropped his gaze to his beer glass instead. 'I was rude to that girl. It was because of what we were talking about in Charleville.'

'What do you mean?'

'I reckon I've forgotten what my Meggie looked like. I never had a photo of her. Only thing I've got to remind me is that letter and my cup and clock.' He gestured to the box on the chair. 'That's why I left them at home until my last night. Meggie liked to drink her tea out of fine china, so she left one of her cups at my place. I always drink my tea out of it. Might look like a bit of a pansy, but it reminds me of her.'

'What about the clock?' Callie asked gently.

'She gave it to me for my birthday, the first three months we were going out. I was always late and I didn't wear a watch back then, so she bought me that clock.'

'She liked fine old things.'

'She did.' Reg's laugh was bitter. 'Maybe if she'd hung around, she would have liked me more. I'm an old thing now.'

'A fine, old thing,' Callie said putting her hand on his.

'I was rude to that girl because it's a problem with an old mind, pulling out dreams, instead of reality.'

'What do you mean?'

'When I saw her standing there on my veranda. I thought it was my Meggie come back. I thought she looked just like her. Same dark, curly hair, same eyes, same pretty mouth. She came out of my dreams. It wasn't her, was it?'

'No, it wasn't. But I think your house has a lovely new owner. When they get up and going, I'll take you out there for a cup of tea one day.'

Reg nodded slowly. 'I'd like that. A man can dream.'

Callie couldn't help herself. She held the table, stood and walked around to the other side of the table where Reg was sitting. She leaned down and brushed her lips across his cheek. 'You take care of yourself,' she said softly. 'Braden just turned down towards the school. I'll walk down and meet him. I'll get him to drop your bag and suitcase here before he drives my car out to *Kilcoy*. It'll give him the opportunity to have a beer, I guess,' she added cheekily.

Chapter 13

Jenna stood on the newly-sanded floorboards on the front veranda and looked out over her acre. It was amazing what a difference three weeks made. She had spent a fortune at the local hardware store, and the truck had come out to *'Margie's Cottage Café'*, as she started to think of her new venture, at least a dozen times delivering timber, paint, sandpaper, roller brushes, paint trays, nails, and, with one big splurge, she'd even bought a ready-made Kaboodle kitchen.

The new stove, dishwasher, and coffee machine were in boxes stored in the back bedroom. As they'd stripped rooms and pulled out cupboards, she'd found quite a few of Mr MacGilvray's possessions and had packed them carefully into a box to take to him when he'd moved into the aged care facility.

A local handyman had called in to see if she had any work going; Kirk had proved a godsend. Not only had he provided a third set of hands with the inside work; he had been a fabulous help in the garden. He had all the tools needed for clearing and a huge mower, and the acre was already looking like a picture with the freshly mowed lawns. He also had plumbing skills and the customer powder room was almost complete. Jenna had decided to convert the sleepout on the side veranda. It was coming together quickly, and she was really happy with their progress.

She smiled as she watched Kirk talking to Alana down near the mulch heap. Alana had been *very* happy when she'd hired the good-looking young man.

Callie had called in a few times to see how they were going, and now Jenna walked to the stairs as she spotted the four-wheel drive come up the newly surfaced driveway. Another woman was driving, and when she stepped out of the car, she went around to the passenger side and helped Callie out.

They walked across the new driveway together.

'Hi, Jenna. Wow, the place is looking fabulous. You certainly have a magic touch,' Callie said.

'Thank you. I'm really happy with what we've achieved this week especially. How are you, Callie? You've grown even bigger since last week when you called in.'

'I know! How much bigger can I get? Jenna, this is my sister-in-law, Sophie. Braden insisted she drove us in this morning. We've dropped the boys off to school, and caught up with some friends in town.'

Sophie waved her hand. 'Welcome to town, Jenna. I can't believe what you've done. This place is going to be a showpiece. Once you get your signs out the front, you'll be pretty busy.'

'Thank you. We've had so much support and help, it's been overwhelming. Even as far as Charleville, plus the lady from the Morven Information Centre called me yesterday asking for brochures. The Charleville Information Centre gave her my contact details.'

'And don't forget the north. Send some to Tambo and Blackall as well,' Sophie said.

'And Barcaldine,' Callie chipped in.

'And if you need more help when you open, give me a call,' Sophie added. 'I'd be happy to volunteer a couple of days a week when you open. I'll give you my mobile number. I'll be driving the boys to school once Callie has the bub.'

'For a couple of weeks,' Callie protested.

'We'll see.' Sophie grinned.

Jenna thought Sophie seemed lovely. How kind to offer to volunteer. 'I might take you up on that offer.'

'Please do.'

'Between my husband and my sister-in-law, my life is organised for me!' Callie shook her head. 'Anyway, we just called in to drop this off.' Callie reached into her bag and passed a folded piece of paper to Jenna. 'It's an invitation to the get-together next Sunday at the park. It's going to be a big day.'

'We'll be there. Callie, while I think of it, I've been putting Mr MacGilvray's stuff into a box. I've found quite a few of his things. Do you think he'd mind if I visited him?'

'I'm sure Reg would love it. He's moved

into the home, but it's probably best to visit him at the pub. You can always find him sitting at the table outside the side door.'

'Will he be at the get-together?'

'I hadn't thought of that, but I'll make sure he is. I'll see you there.'

'You won't be in hospital by then, will you?'

Callie laughed. 'Don't you start! The whole family have a bet going that when I go to the obstetrician next week, he's going to send me to the hospital in Charleville. I'm not going to miss the welcome picnic. I've instructed the baby to stay there until after next Sunday.'

Jenna put her hands up and chuckled. 'I won't take sides. You just stay healthy and have that baby soon!'

'Okay, we'll see you Sunday.'

'Yes. Nice to meet you, Sophie, and thank you for your offer. Alana and I are off to

Charleville soon to collect some furniture. Kirk's cleared a spot under the side veranda to put some tables.'

'I was pleased to see you hired Kirk. He's a dynamo,' Callie said.

'He's fabulous.'

'And very easy on the eye.' Sophie chuckled.

'Alana noticed that the minute he arrived here looking for work.'

'How long do you think it will be before you open?' Sophie asked as Jenna walked across to the car with them.

'The plan is for another three weeks, but we won't advertise until we're certain we can do it.'

'Did you get the flyers done?' Callie asked.

'We're picking them up today.'

'Sounds great. See you soon.'

Jenna smiled as she watched Sophie help

Callie into the high car. The more time she spent here, the happier she was.

'Alana,' she called. 'Are you ready to go to Charleville?'

Chapter 14

Warrego River Campground -Sunday

Jenna and Alana walked from the car park behind the pub to the picnic site by the river just before midday on Sunday. As they crossed the road, Kirk's blue ute came around the corner and he parked about fifty metres up the road.

'I'll see you in a while, Jen. I'll just go and say hello to Kirk.'

Alana had been a tremendous help, and she seemed as happy as Jenna was. Kirk was a lovely guy and he seemed smitten with Alana too. Jenna just hoped it didn't go pear-shaped before the opening. She couldn't afford to lose either of them.

As she watched, Kirk climbed out of his ute and held his hand out to Alana with a big smile.

So far, things were looking rosy.

A big marquee was set up under the trees near the river, with three smaller tents beside it. Happy squeals came from a jumping castle in the middle of the flat park. A man led a child around on a small pony, and Jenna noticed a queue of children behind the roped-off area. At the far end of the grassy park, three caravans filled the space under the hill. The smell of barbequing meat and onions drifted across and Jenna's stomach rumbled.

'Jenna!'

She turned as her name was called. Sophie was walking across the grass towards her.

'Hi, Sophie. Looks like you've got a good crowd here already.'

'We have, but mostly locals so far. There are

a few new arrivals over near the drinks tent, and they're getting to know each other. Come with me, and I'll introduce you. But first the local brigade.'

A group of women manned a table in next to the barbeque. Rows of buttered bread and sauce bottles filled the table. A tall good-looking man wearing an apron manned the grill.

'Hi everyone,' Sophie called out. 'This is Jenna, the already famous Jenna of *Margie's Cottage Café*. Jenna, you won't remember all the names, but this is Amelia and Laura, and Dr Harry is the one in the sexy apron.'

The man flipping steaks on the barbeque smiled. 'Welcome, Jenna.'

She smiled shyly.

'And this is Kimberley. She's deputy at the primary school.'

'Hi, Jenna. Are you going to do coffee deliveries? I have a captive clientele for you at the school.'

Jenna shook her head. 'I hadn't even thought of that.'

'Worth considering.'

'I'll give it some thought.'

Sophie put her arm through Jenna's and they walked across to the drinks tent. A couple were chatting at the front and they both turned with a smile.

'This is Fallon and Jon. Guys, meet Jenna.'

'Hi, Jenna. This is my mum, Ruth,' Fallon said nodding to the older woman holding a baby. Another woman behind the counter turned around and waved. 'Welcome to town, I'm Bec, and the guy setting up the microphone is Matt.'

'I'm overwhelmed,' Jenna said. 'Please forgive me if I call you the wrong name.'

'I told you we should have had name tags, Sophie.'

Jenna turned as she recognised Callie's voice.

'Hi, Callie. That's one name I do know.'

A tall man with a rugged face had his arm around Callie.

'Jenna, this is my husband, Braden, and the three terrors over there looking at the cake stall are Rory, Nigel, and Petie.'

'Good to meet you, Jenna,' Braden said. 'Callie, we gave up waiting for the horse ride. Petie can go later. I'll grab your chair out of the car. Where do you want me to put it?'

'Can you get both chairs please, love? Reg agreed to come across as long as he could sit near the beer tent, so put them over there.'

'Will do, and then I'll go over and prise him from his table at the pub.'

Jenna noticed the way Callie and Braden's eyes connected and a message passed between them.

'I'll take Petie with me, okay?' Braden said.

'That would be good. I'll organise drinks and cake for the boys. Jenna, everything has been donated so don't try to pay for anything.'

'Come with me, Jenna. I'll take you over to the new group and you can learn some more names,' Sophie said.

Jenna smiled at the people she'd met. 'Great to meet you all. I'd love to chat later.' She followed Sophie across the grass.

Sophie lowered her voice. 'Callie's a bit on edge because the last time we were all together, there was an accident and Petie ended up in hospital in Brisbane for a few weeks. He's fine now, thanks to Matt who saved him, but Braden and Callie are very protective.'

'Understandably,' Jenna commented.

'It happened at our wedding, but all's well now. Come and meet my husband, Kent, and then we'll go over to the new group. I'm going to go and rustle up some name tags!'

Jenna spent the next hour chatting to the other new arrivals in town. Alana joined them, and Kirk went over to the beer tent to help out.

Everyone seemed really nice, and there were a lot of comments about how good it was to see new businesses coming to town. Three of the other new arrivals had started innovative agricultural projects, and there were two new nurses at the hospital, as well as a new casual teacher at the school.

Jenna excused herself and walked across the grass to the beer tent. She'd noticed that Reg had arrived and was sitting in one of the chairs that Braden had set up. There was no sign of Callie and Jenna frowned.

'Hello, Mr MacGilvray,' she said when she reached him. He looked up at her and his eyes widened.

'It's Reg. No one calls me that. Mr

MacGilvray was my father. God rest his soul.'

'Is Callie all right?' she asked looking around.

'She's gone to the ladies' room,' he said gruffly looking away from her.

'May I sit with you for a while? I'd like to talk to you.'

He shrugged, but Jenna sat in the empty chair. 'I'll go when Callie comes back.'

Someone had placed a table in front of the two chairs, and a pot of tea and a bowl of sugar sat next to a plate of different types of cake slices.

'Do you want a cup of tea if you're going to chat?' Reg asked placing his cup on the table.

'That would be good, thank you. I'll go and find a cup.'

'No, stay there' He jumped to his feet, very sprightly for a man his age. 'I'll get one for you.'

'Thank you.'

Reg disappeared into the crowd and Jenna looked at the cup on the table, her eyes narrowing. She reached over and picked it up. The cup was burgundy on the outside with a gold handle; the inside was stained almost black. There was no saucer.

She frowned; she was sure there was a set in that same colour with gold handles in Gran's timber box; she'd have a look when she was at the cottage tomorrow. That was another job to add to her list now that the kitchen was almost finished. Wash up all the fine china and put it in the new cupboards.

And hand wash, not put them in the dishwasher. Gran would turn in her grave.

Jenna spotted Reg coming back, and she put the cup back on the table, but he obviously had good eyesight.

'Why were you looking at my cup?' He put

a plain white teacup in front of her and sat down. 'I don't clean the inside because it makes the tea taste better.'

'Oh, I was just looking at it because I think I have some with the same pattern in the cottage.'

'Probably some modern copy,' he said picking the teapot up. 'Did you want milk because I'll have to go and get some if you want white tea.'

'No, black is fine, thank you.'

He poured her tea, refilled his own cup and picked it up. 'Mine is an *original* cup.'

'Mine are too,' she said.

He stared at her. 'Where did you get them from? I didn't think girls these days liked old-fashioned things.'

'They were my gran's. She came from Augathella. That's one of the reasons I moved here.'

Reg stared at her. 'What was her name?'

146

'Margaret.'

'Margaret who?'

'Margaret Hope.'

'And she's your grandmother, you said?' His voice seemed forced.

'Yes.'

'I think I remember a Margaret Hope. What can you tell me about her? Where is she now?'

'Gran passed away three years ago.' Jenna blinked tears away; it still hurt.

Reg made a strange sound. 'Was she happy?'

'She was. Did you really know her before she moved away?'

'I think so. My old memory's not real good these days,' he said. 'Tell me a bit about her.'

'She moved to Brisbane when she was nineteen and she did dressmaking. She loved all the vintage stuff, the old clothes, the fine china, and I inherited the same interests. I miss her so much. She was my best friend.'

'What about your grandfather?' he asked slowly. 'Is he still around?'

'I never had one. Gran was a single mum. She only ever had my mum.'

'I think you look like her.'

'My mum always said that. So, you do remember her?'

'Aye, lass. I do. Where is your mother?' His voice was shaky, and Jenna wondered if he was sick.

She looked over at him, and he was watching her intently. 'Mum and Dad live in a caravan, and they are travelling around Australia. Why do you want to know?'

'I just wondered if your mother ever came back here to visit. I might have met her.'

'I don't think so. But they will come and visit when I open the tea shop.'

'How old is your mother?'

What a strange question from a stranger.

Reg's eyes were wide and his hands were shaking.

'Are you okay?' she asked, concerned.

'How old is your mother?' he insisted.

'Mum's fifty-four next month. She was born in 1969 on the day Neil Armstrong walked on the moon.'

Reg jumped up and picked up his cup. 'Nice talking to you, girl. I'll see you around.'

Jenna shook her head as he disappeared into the crowd.

What a strange man.

Chapter 15

Jenna sat at the table for about ten minutes after Reg left, and then she looked around with a frown; Callie was a long time coming back from the ladies' room. Maybe she'd got talking to somebody on the way back.

Jenna stood and walked around looking through the crowd; there must be over two hundred people here. She went in the beer tent and the barbeque tent and then looked over to where the children were lined up waiting for a horse ride. She also glanced over at the playground.

There was no one at the unmanned cake

stall as all the cakes were gone. The group of new people that had been over towards the river had joined in with the main crowd, and most people were sitting at tables along the grassed flat.

Braden was holding a small boy's hand as they waited for a ride on the Shetland pony, she guessed it was Petie. There was no sign of Callie. Jenna didn't want to worry anyone, so she decided to go and have a look in the restroom near the road before she asked if anyone knew where Callie was.

The building was about a hundred metres from the picnic ground and she walked over looking around the park. She walked around to the front of the concrete building; it smelled of disinfectant and was spotlessly clean.

As she entered the dark interior, Jenna called out, 'Callie, are you in here?'

The answer came first in the form of a

ragged groan, and she ran inside. The door to one of the cubicles was closed.

'Callie, are you in there?' she yelled out.

'Yes, Jenna, it's me. Thank God you're here. I need help. I'm stuck.' Callie's voice broke. 'The baby's coming. I need help. Can you get the door unlocked? I'm on the floor with my back against it.'

Jenna pulled her phone out of her pocket. 'I've got my phone here. I'll call an ambulance and then I'll run over to Braden.' She thought quickly; she couldn't leave Callie here by herself. She sounded terrified.

'No, better still, I'll call an ambulance, and then I'll call Alana to get her to tell Brayden.'

'Oh, thank you. I feel so much better now. I knew someone would come in here eventually, but it's been ages, and the concrete is so cold on my bottom, and my waters have broken, and I'm sitting in a pool of water. *Argghh!* Another contraction's coming!'

Callie's deep groan made goosebumps rise on Jenna's skin. Someone had to hear her across the field.

Her groaning ended and Callie was quiet for a moment then she panted out, 'Jenna, the contractions are only a couple of minutes apart and awfully strong. I'm terrified the baby's going to be born here in the bloody public toilet in Augathella.'

'It won't be, Callie, Trust me. Keep talking to me while I make a call.'

Jenna dialled triple zero, and once she'd chosen ambulance from the selection, the operator picked up straight away.

'I'm at Augathella, and there's a pregnant woman in labour in the public toilet at Riverside Park,' Jenna said quickly.

'Is there any sign of the baby coming yet?' the operator asked.

'Yes.' Callie groaned from behind the door. 'Yes, I think the birth is imminent.'

'I need you to answer some questions for me, and then we'll get some help on the way. First what's your name, and what is the exact address of where you are.'

Once the details were given, the operator spoke again. 'Okay, this is what I need you to do, Jenna.'

Jenna replied urgently. 'I can't do anything; Callie's locked in a cubicle. I'm going to get help. Please send an ambulance.'

'Callie, they're sending an ambulance now. It's okay. I'm on the phone.' Jenna disconnected from the operator, then called Alana's number. 'Answer, Alana, please answer.' The phone rang out, and then Jenna remembered that she had Sophie's number; she had given it to her the other day in case she decided she would need her help. She searched for it on her contacts and when she pressed call it picked up straight away.

'Hello?' Sophie answered.

'Thank God, Sophie. It's me, Jenna!'

'Jenna, where are you?'

'I'm over in the restroom with Callie. The one across the park. She's gone into labour.'

'Oh my God,' Sophie said. 'I'm on my way.'

'I've called an ambulance. Can you bring Braden?'

'Yes, and I'll get Dr Harry and Laura too. She's a midwife. We've got lots of help here. Stay there, Jenna. We'll be there in about two minutes.'

Callie groaned again, and this time it rose to a scream. Jenna felt absolutely useless with the closed door between them. She got down on her knees and looked underneath the door that hung a few centimetres above the concrete. She reached her hand through and felt around, touching Callie's back.

'I'm here, Callie, and help is on the way. Can you just hang on for another minute or two?'

Callie started panting. 'Oh my God, Jenna, I don't know if I can. This is nothing like the classes that Braden and I went to. This is what it's supposed to feel like at the end of labour, not at the beginning. I don't know what to do. I can't have our baby here.'

'Hang in there, Callie. Help is coming. Dr Harry will be here in a minute and Laura.

She could hear voices and she jumped to her feet stood and hurried to the door. 'We're in here!'

Braden's face was set and pale as he rushed to the door. The man who had been wearing the apron at the barbeque was behind him.

'Thank goodness,' Jenna said. 'The door's

locked from the inside. Callie's on the floor and she can't reach the lock.'

'We'll sort it. Thanks, Jenna,' Braden said as he ran past her. 'We're here, love. It's going to be okay.'

Relief flooded through Jenna. Callie was in good hands now. Her hands started shaking as reaction set in.

The doctor went inside after Braden and they were followed in by the pretty woman with the long braid. Laura, the midwife.

'Callie, look up,' Braden said. 'I'm going to climb over the top of the stall from this side. Then we can open the door.'

'Thank goodness the door opens outwards,' Dr Harry said.

There was little sound as Sophie and Jenna moved outside.

'I'll wait here with you, Sophie' Jenna said. 'I feel totally useless.'

'Don't be silly. You called for help,' Sophie reassured her. 'I'd better go back and check on Petie.' Her forehead wrinkled in a frown. 'But I don't want to leave here.'

Jenna shook her head. 'Look, you stay here. I can go and watch Petie. Is Petie the little boy who was queued up with Braden for the horse ride?'

'Yes, he's with Amelia now. Do you remember meeting her?'

'Yes, I do. She was the one that had the dog with her, Chilli. She introduced me to him when I went back to the tent after I met the other new people.'

'Yes, that's Amelia. Can you just make sure Petie's okay and stays in the tent? We are very, very careful with him since the accident.'

'I will. Should I tell anyone what's going on? They'll wonder when they see the ambulance arrive.'

'I'm sure Callie won't mind. Just don't worry the three boys.'

'I'll be careful what I say if they ask.'

Jenna took off across the field and was soon at the beer tent. She looked around for Petie; he was sitting at the back of the tent playing with Chilli, the dog. She sat down beside Amelia and told her what was going on.

'Oh no, it's sort of good news and bad,' Amelia said. I know Callie wanted to get the birth over and done with but not here at the park. At least Harry and Laura are here today.'

'They're with her now. And Braden and Sophie. Sophie was worried about Petie.'

'Yes, I'll never forget that afternoon at their wedding. We'll make sure he doesn't get into any trouble. Actually, you sit here with Ben and Petie and I'll go and get Rory and Nigel. Are you going to tell them what's happening?'

'No, not just yet.'

Amelia stood. 'Oh, I don't think you've met Ben, have you?'

'No, I didn't. Hello, Ben.' Jenna sent him a brief smile.

'You'll be getting to know Ben soon,' Amelia said. 'He's a local building inspector.'

Jenna nodded. 'I'm almost ready for you, Ben.' She squeezed her hands together. Callie had been in such distress; it really worried her. She was supposed to go to Charleville and have the baby because she was so big.

'It's okay, Jenna. Don't worry. Callie's in the best hands. We're very lucky to have Doc and Laura in town.'

Chapter 16

Reg put his head into his hands and groaned. He sat at the table that filled the small window alcove in his new room. He'd unpacked his precious box and his cup and clock took pride of place in the centre of the table. His thoughts were in turmoil about what Jenna had said.

He hadn't been wrong.

His reaction when he'd spotted her on the veranda of his house the other day had been right. She was the image of his Meggie, and she had to be her granddaughter.

The big question was, was she also *his* granddaughter? Her mother had been born in July 1969. The dates lined up perfectly. Meggie had spent the night at his house four times in late October and November 1968. He remembered well; because the first time had been for his birthday on the twenty-eighth of October that year; she'd cooked him a roast dinner. They'd sat outside and looked at the stars and then she had stayed the night. The first night she had slept in his bed was imprinted in his memory. Meggie's birthday was in November and she'd stayed that night, plus two more nights that month after the Saturday night dance. She wasn't seeing anyone else. He knew that.

It had been the end of November when he'd driven the truck to Darwin for Horrie Andersen and when he came home just before Christmas, Meggie was gone.

All that was there waiting for him was the letter she'd left him.

And now Meggie was truly gone. She'd

been gone three years and he hadn't even known.

Reg looked down with surprise as a wet drop landed on the table in front of him. He reached up and touched his eyes; tears were streaming down his cheeks.

His Meggie was dead. He'd never seen her again.

And now I never will.

Had she known she was pregnant when she left? How the heck was he going to find out, or was he just being a silly old man? Should he just let it go?

He'd gone his whole life without knowing that he had a daughter and a granddaughter; why should he change now?

What a waste he had made of his life. He had done nothing memorable; shorn a few thousand sheep, driven a truck and fallen in love with his beautiful Meggie. Somehow, she'd decided that she didn't want to be with him.

He'd spent the rest of his life sitting at the pub hoping Meggie would come looking for him.

Reg opened his wallet and carefully pulled out the letter and read it for probably the five thousandth time in his life. Even when he'd first read it all those years ago, he'd had no idea what it really meant. He knew that she loved him; she'd told him so many times. And she wouldn't have slept with him if she hadn't, would she?

Meggie had known that he loved her much more than he'd ever loved the bush. He would have followed her to the ends of the earth. He would have lived in a hippie commune if that's what she'd wanted.

Maybe he should talk to Callie and get a woman's point of view about the letter and what her words actually meant. Was he not reading enough into them? Had he always missed the meaning behind the words? Was there a hidden message he'd missed?

He should have gone to Brisbane and looked for Meggie as soon as he'd got back. But he'd had no idea where to go, and she had specifically told him not to follow her.

He'd drunk himself into oblivion for the first three months. Another tear rolled down his cheek, and Reg was disgusted in himself; always had been, always would be. He was an absolute waste of space.

He wanted to go to sleep tonight and not wake up. At least it would free up the room for some other sad bugger.

Chapter 17

Callie sat up in the bed of the maternity ward at their local hospital. Harry had decreed that they didn't have time to either wait for the ambulance or take her to Charleville. By the time Braden had climbed over and opened the door, Sophie had brought their four-wheel drive onto the park. Kent had come across to help lift Callie into the back seat.

She had been in the delivery room within minutes, and Harry and Laura had been at their professional best.

Braden stood next to the bed looking down at her with tears in his eyes.

'Are you okay, love?' she asked.

He reached down and kissed her. 'Am I okay? I should be asking you that!'

'I'm wonderful. A bit shell-shocked, and amazed that it was all over in less than an hour.'

'You are amazing.'

'Can we call her Meg?' Callie whispered as she looked at the crib at the end of the bed.

'I think that's perfect for her.' Braden reached down and held Callie's hand as though he was never going to let go. His grin was wide as she stared up at him.

'And what about "Muesli"?' he asked looking at the other crib to the side.

'I'll give you "Muesli"! she said laughing.

'What about Munro? Meg and Munro Cartwright?' Braden's lips moved against her forehead.

'I like both,' she said. 'Oh my God, Bray, how am I going to look after two babies? I haven't had any time to get my head around one, let alone twins, and we need so much stuff. Double everything I've bought.'

'We'll sort it. I think you're going to have lots of helpers.'

'I think I'll need them. How could I have not known it was twins?'

'The obstetrician and the ultrasounds didn't even pick it up, so how could you? Harry explained it to me when Laura was weighing them. They were so close together that the smallest baby, in this case, our little Meg, his behind her brother.'

'And as simple as that we now have five children.'

Braden chuckled. 'I'd better go and buy some more cattle to pay the bills. I don't think you'll be going back to work at the school for a while.'

Harry and Laura came to the door, smiles on

both faces.

'How are you feeling, Callie?' Laura asked. 'I have a very happy Auntie Sophie and Uncle Kent out here, and three very excited little boys. Are you up to a visit?'

'I am. And can I have a cup of tea? I missed out at the picnic.'

'I'll make it myself,' Dr Harry said, and he disappeared into the hall.

Callie's heart filled with love as Sophie and Kent, and Rory, Nigel, and Petie came into the room. 'Come and meet your new brother . . . and sister, boys,' she said. 'And Auntie Sophie and Uncle Kent, you now have a new nephew *and* niece.'

The three boys hurried over to the two cribs and Sophie stared at Callie and Braden, her eyes wide with shock.

'Twins? You had twins?'

'We did,' Braden said proudly. 'Your turn

next, Soph.'

'Hmmm. . . we'll see,' Sophie said, looking away.

Chapter 18

Three days later

Jenna had called at the pub three afternoons in a row when she came to town to visit the hardware store. She brought the set of cups that were the same as Reg's with her but wanted to compare them to make sure. She'd taken a photo and done a reverse image search on Google. The set was a Shelley piece called Pink Roses. Inside each of her cups was a bouquet of pink roses and she was going to ask Reg if she could clean his and see if it was the same pattern.

But he hadn't been there. She'd asked Sean at the bistro if he knew where he was, but he shrugged.

'We wondered too, but we figure he has all the company he wants at the home now. But we do miss the old bugger,' Sean said.

'I hope he's not sick,' she said. 'I might go there and see if I can visit him tomorrow.'

The next afternoon, Jenna changed out of her work clothes and scrubbed the paint off her hands. As well as seeing Reg, she'd call in to see Callie at the hospital. Even though it was winter, the day was warm, and she put on her favourite dress. Like the set of Shelley cups, it was patterned with pink roses on a cream background. She left her hair loose and headed to town.

The first stop was to see Callie and the twins. Callie was pleased to see her, but Jenna kept her visit brief as there seemed to be a stream of visitors going in and out. Callie had even made the *Western Times newspaper* with her surprise twins and their birth at the picnic.

'Thanks for coming, Jenna,' Callie said as she made to leave. 'And thank you again for getting me help so quickly.'

'My pleasure. I'm off to visit Reg now. I have a bit of a mystery to solve.'

'A mystery?' Callie asked.

Jenna quickly explained how she had a set of five of her late grandmother's cups, and she suspected that Reg might have the missing sixth.

Callie's eyes widened. 'What was your grandmother's name?'

'Margaret, but she always went by Margie or Meggie.'

'Margaret Hope?' Callie said softly.

Jenna nodded. 'How did you know that? Did Reg tell you I asked him about her?'

'No, but I think you'd better go and talk to him. Go gently with him, Jenna. But I think this might make him very happy,' Callie said enigmatically.

##

Jenna was thoughtful as she walked to the back of the hospital grounds where the aged care facility was situated. Like Reg's box, she carried her precious cups in a small timber box. She pushed open the door and walked across to the desk. Three elderly people were watching television in a large recreation room, but there was no sign of Reg.

'Hello.' The woman at the desk smiled at her. 'How can I help you?'

'I was hoping to visit Mr Reg MacGilvray.'

'Oh, I'm so pleased. He's been really sad since he came to us last week. Are you a relative?'

'I . . . I think I might be,' Jenna said slowly.

'I need to talk to him.'

'He's in his room. I've just taken him a cup of tea in that stained old cup he insists on using. Would you like to have one with him?'

'I would, but could I ask a huge favour? Would you make it in this cup?' She opened the box and passed a china teacup to the carer.

'Of course. I'll bring it down. He's in room six at the end of the hall. Just go down and tap on his door and open it. He might be dozing.'

Jenna carried the box under her arm and walked down the hall. The strangest feeling filled her chest and her hands felt light as she took in deep breaths, not knowing what to say to him.

Jenna tapped gently on the door, and a gruff voice called, 'Come in.'

She turned the knob and pushed open the door, balancing the box in her other hand. Reg was sitting at a table by the window looking out onto a pretty rose garden. 'Hello . . . Mr MacGilvray.'

'Reg, please.'

She walked over slowly and put the box on the table and looked down at him. His face was unshaven, and his eyes were shadowed, and even though it was two in the afternoon, he was wearing blue-striped pyjamas.

Before she could speak again, there was a tap on the door and the carer came in with Jenna's cup of tea.

When she placed the cup on the table, Reg's eyes widened. The woman looked at each of them, and sensing the emotion in the room, she left and closed the door quietly behind her.

Jenna sat down and picked up her teacup. She took a sip. Her voice shook as she looked at him, and saw the tears forming in his eyes. Eyes that she now recognised as being very much like her mother's.

She cleared her throat, which felt thick and heavy. 'Instead of calling you Reg, I think I would like to call you Grandfather. You knew as soon as you saw me that day, didn't you?'

Tears rolled down his unshaven cheeks as he held her eyes. 'Aye, I did, lass. I did. You are the image of your grandmother.'

She nodded and her tears spilled over. 'I know.'

'My Meggie.' Reg reached into the pocket of his pyjama shirt and pulled out a clean handkerchief. As he leaned over and wiped Jenna's tears away, his touch was gentle.

THE END

To be continued in An Augathella Baby

Available in print at Annie's store:

https://www.annieseaton.net/store.html

OTHER BOOKS

Whitsunday Dawn
Undara
Osprey Reef
East of Alice

Porter Sisters Series

Kakadu Sunset
Daintree
Diamond Sky
Hidden Valley
Larapinta
Kakadu Dawn

Pentecost Island Series

Pippa
Eliza
Nell
Tamsin
Evie
Cherry
Odessa
Sienna
Tess
Isla

Also available in three boxed sets
Books 1-3
Books 4-6
Books 7-10

The Augathella Girls Series

Outback Roads
Outback Sky
Outback Escape
Outback Wind
Outback Dawn
Outback Moonlight
Outback Dust
Outback Hope

Sunshine Coast Series

Waiting for Ana
The Trouble with Jack
Healing His Heart
Sunshine Coast Boxed Set

The Richards Brothers Series

The Trouble with Paradise
Marry in Haste
Outback Sunrise
Richards Brothers Boxed Set

Bondi Beach Love Series

Beach House
Beach Music
Beach Walk
Beach Dreams
The House on the Hill

Second Chance Bay Series

Her Outback Playboy
Her Outback Protector
Her Outback Haven

About the Author

Annie lives in Australia, on the beautiful north coast of New South Wales. She sits in her writing chair and looks out over the tranquil Pacific Ocean.

She writes contemporary romance and loves telling stories that always have a happily ever after. She lives with her very own hero of many years and they share their home with Toby, the naughtiest dog in the universe, and Barney, the ragdoll puss, who hides when the four grandchildren come to visit.

Stay up to date with her latest releases at her website: http://www.annieseaton.net